DEATH OF THE FRENCHMAN

B.B. Boudreau

Death of the Frenchman

Copyright © 2020 by Barbara Boudreau
All rights reserved.
No part of this book may be reproduced in whole or in part without written permission from the publisher, except by reviewers who may quote brief excerpts in connection with a review.

ISBN-13: 978-0-578-61745-9
This book is a work of fiction, and any resemblance to persons living or dead is purely coincidental.

Death of the Frenchman

by B.B. Boudreau

B.B. Boudreau

Death of the Frenchman

Author's Notes

I wrote *Death of the Frenchman* during National Novel Writing Month (NaNoWriMo) in 2012, one the most difficult years of my life. I submitted to spinal fusion surgery in March, and battled through a long, painful recovery that often left me gasping for breath. Then in July my mother had a hip replacement and tumbled from the cliff of her former life into the grip of Alzheimer's. We brought her to our home in September, and our life became a trio. Despite the Alzheimer's, Marjorie Buls was an easy roommate, apart from her tendency to wander, which was terrifying at times and eventually led to admission in an Assisted Care unit. My former active life was rendered sedentary by these factors, and writing became a much needed escape into my imagination. A sequel to *The Frenchman* was essential; though the story had "ended," the question kept coming from readers: "But what happened to them?" I myself wondered late at night during the futile battle for sleep, willing the pain away, ears perked for sounds of my mother's stirrings. Though *The Frenchman* was complete, the story was unfinished.

On November 1, I fired up my laptop, poised my hands over the keyboard and began to sculpt the sequel of Jean, Lilly, Henry, Amos, Sherri and Guy Santino. The imposed schedule kept me on track, and I successfully completed the NaNoWriMo goal of 50,000 words in 30 days. It was great fun.

Mom passed in 2015 and I still hear her words, "What are you doing?" as I pecked away from my station on the sofa. Although she never got the chance to read it, she was my impetus for completing the story. My never ending thanks to the beautiful woman who gave me life.

A huge debt of gratitude to my husband and best friend Al, and to my loyal Aussie Shepherd Lila, who at 16 years old will likely not live to see another novel of my creation.

They certainly know who I am.

Last but certainly not least, thank you to The Finish Line writers group; Jane, Cindys 1 & 2, Sandra, Ann, Terry and Dan. You are my haven from the storm, my rock in bumpy seas.

Every writer needs one.

Chapter 1

September, mid-90s — a tropical island off the coast of Venezuela

A pair of stocky bare feet padded down the center of the dirt road that led back from the village. Soundless sunrise glanced off the boy's wild curls. A ten-pound grouper hanging from a stringer over his shoulder bounced against his back with each step, the bulbous ebony eye echoing the red-orange globe growing over the long horizon of ocean. His mother would be pleased. Grouper was a delectable first-choice fish on the island. The catch had taken only twenty minutes, leaving more time for morning chores.

Henry dumped the fish in the deep sink outside the kitchen door and climbed the inside stairs, rapping softly on his parents' bedroom door.

The knock stole LaChance's dream of dripping spring Parisian streets. It was the only place he went in his dreams.

But nothing in life was better than waking up here. Jean LaChance had woken up in many different beds in his life. Until now. He inhaled the scent of his wife's black curls on the pillow beside his. He shifted in the bed, stirring little Evie awake where she was wedged between them. She turned her round head, carpeted with peach fuzz, took one look at the man who was the center of her existence, and smiled. That smile, that light that was everything. Another perfect morning.

He reminisced as he sometimes did on perfect mornings after a dream of France; back to the years of his former life. Practicality had demanded an existence with no ethical context. He had had control—period. Over years of survival and conquest, his life became formidable; he was armored and safe and unavailable for emotion he had considered a waste of time. Emotion was weakness. He had been tough, relentless, stoic to the point of loneliness, though he would have denied it. Nothing had bothered him.

And now, the smile of a fifteen-month-old child undid him.

Evie opened her mouth in a primal screech. She clapped her hands together and waved them in the air. Jean LaChance, former professional thief, career criminal, drew the baby into his arms and babbled like an animated teddy bear. Evie laughed harder and reached up to grab his exaggerated nose with chubby fingers, her eyes throwing back the sunrise.

The hair on the other side of the big bed stirred, followed by Lilly's reproach. She turned toward them.

"Bon jour," she said softly. "You're winding her up."

"Bon jour, cheri," he answered. "I can't help myself. She's a vixen."

"Let's hope that stops very soon, Jean," Lilly said, and kissed him firmly on the mouth. "I love you, you know."

"Of course I know. I love you too."

Evie gurgled and screamed, sandwiched in-between the couple who for a moment had lost focus on her.

"Oh, Evie!" Jean shushed. "You know that I love you, maybe even as much as I love your mother."

"Fat chance," Lilly said. "You love me more than anybody."

"I don't know, Lilly. Your daughter is giving you a run for your money."

"Nice. Using English clichés for your own benefit. Thanks."

Lilly grabbed her pillow and round-housed it over to the other side of the bed, catching Jean full in the face. He laughed and flung the pillow to the floor. He grabbed Lilly and planted a strong, morning-breath kiss on her mouth. She giggled and landed a gentle slap across his face.

"You're a smitten man, you know that, don't you?"

"Smitten, to the core," Jean answered. He buried his whiskers into the baby's stomach. Her shrieks escalated into high gear.

"You two," Lilly groaned, and vaulted out of bed. "I need a cup of coffee."

"I'll take my coffee in here, dear," Jean said and turned his full attention to the laughing baby.

"I'll see what I can do."

She stood silhouetted in the morning light, hands on her hips, annoyed and adoring at the same time, realizing that she had lost her man to their fifteen-month-old daughter. Prior to Evie's birth, he had been all hers.

"You two are ridiculous," she chided, and turned toward the kitchen. Jean jumped up, leaving the laughing child buried in the bed clothes, swinging her head wildly in an abandoned frenzy.

Lilly almost made it out the bedroom door when Jean caught her, twirled her around and pinned her in his arms. The kiss was filled with fire and as long as either could bear it. Finally, Lilly pushed him out to arm's length and held him there.

"Why are you so irresistible?" she asked.

"Is this a complaint?"

"Not really. Just not used to being trumped by a baby."

"Ah, Lilly, Lilly, Lilly. Don't you realize that loving Evie is loving you?"

The look of his eyes made her pelvis clench. He could always do that.

"Okay, go back to her then. I have work to do."

Lilly freed herself from Jean's arms and started toward the kitchen.

Jean swept the smiling baby off the bed and cartwheeled her in the air.

"Come, little one. Let's change your nappy."

The changing table stood just outside the bedroom door along a wall avalanching baby paraphernalia; powder, wipes, diapers of several varieties, books, toys, and pacifiers. He laid Evie on the table talking nonsense to the child, who hung on every word from the big man's pursed lips. Within seconds, he had stripped the wet diaper from his baby and replaced it with a fresh one. Evie giggled and reached for his hands.

Henry's face peeked around the corner.

"Morning, Dad," he said.

"Good morning, buddy," the man answered, and reached down to caress the boy's shoulder.

"You want me to take Evie?" the boy asked.

"Sure. I'll go help your mother."

Henry lifted the child like an expert parent onto one hip, talking to her like she was an adult. Even at twelve, he was already turning the corner to manhood. He had always been ahead of life's clock.

"Evie, want to go out and look at the ocean? It's a nice day. Maybe we'll see some dolphins."

They disappeared around the corner and Jean turned his attention to Lilly. Brewing coffee was already sending its heady aroma through the house. Jean stepped into the kitchen and pressed up against her back. They swayed from side to side in an erotic dawn dance lit by the flood of sunlight through an east window.

"Have I been good to you?" he asked.

"Ha! Of course you've been good to me. I'm just reserving a little feminine jealousy for my own ego."

Jean took a deep breath of her hair. He let it out slowly.
"Henry called me Dad again."
"That's nice," Lilly said. "How does that feel?"
He breathed in deeply again and hugged her closer.
"It's . . . it's . . . I can't describe it. It's wonderful," he finished.
"It is wonderful," Lilly said. They stood clutched together at the window, their skin pumpkin ginger in the sunrise. "I haven't heard him use that word in – years. I still haven't heard him call you that."

Jean lowered his chin onto her left shoulder. The coffee maker gurgled its last breath, and Lilly unwrapped Jean's arms and opened the cupboard with the mugs.

"What are you doing today, honey?" she asked, knowing that the answer would be an exact copy of yesterday, the day before and days before that.

"We have some new guests coming in, yes?" he asked. Lilly nodded.

"I have to run to the airport in the afternoon, but first, we have to look at the cistern again."

"Do you know where it's leaking?" she asked.

"No, Ramón hasn't figured it out yet. I hope we don't have to bring in a technician. That could be expensive. But we have to fix it. We're losing gallons of water every day."

"It's a good thing it's been raining."

Lilly poured two cups of coffee and handed one to Jean. They clinked the cups together in silence, sending ripples through the foam ring atop the strong black liquid.

"If you get the fruit ready, I'll start toast," she said, and popped his rear.

Their house was set a bit apart from the guest house with a privacy screen of flaming bougainvillea in between. Currently, there were ten clients in the guest house bedrooms, five couples with the flavor of a United Nations convention: two Americans, two French, two Germans, two Japanese and two Spaniards.

Business was moderate, yet steady, and they had settled into the proprietor role like seasoned hotel owners. Jean maintained the building and the infrastructure and Lilly provided comfort; bedding, food, amenities, including chocolates on the pillows of new arrivals. Clients booked up to two weeks in the comfy guest house, and Lilly and Jean supplied a homey touch, complete with children who all shared in the chores. The guest house was functional, yet it was an old building, with all the headaches of aging tropical real estate; leaking roofs, peeling paint, ancient wiring, cracked floor tiles and antiquated plumbing begging for a refit. Despite all the daily challenges, even after two years, Jean and Lilly were still on a magic carpet gliding through paradise, a place where no misfortune could disrupt their idyllic world.

Those two years had raced by, and his life before his time with Lilly was a shadow. A solo existence had fit him well. Jean LaChance had been a loner from the start—abandoned in an orphanage after losing his mother at age nine. In this life, he was Pierre LaPorte—businessman, husband, daddy. Everyday centered on caring for other people. Complete metamorphosis.

Jean stood at the kitchen counter near the window overlooking the sweep of palm trees descending to the ocean half a mile away. The ripe neon-orange papayas slipped through his fingers, cleaving under the light pressure of the paring knife. Fresh fruit was available nearly all year, depending on the season, and provided a rare treat for northern guests. The property held a dozen tropical fruit trees: oranges, tangerines, papayas, mangoes, avocados, lemons and limes all grew within a short distance of the house. The three older kids were responsible for the harvest as well as farm chores including feeding the small flock of chickens, gathering eggs, and grooming and milking their cow, Sadie, purchased last year from a local farmer. The kids had grown since their arrival, and had eased into island life. Jean spoiled them all, to Lilly's disapproval, but even she realized they deserved a bit of spoiling.

Jean was the first real father Sherri could remember. Although Henry did remember the long-gone John Parsons, he refused to talk about the man who had abandoned them when he was only eight years old. That life was over. This one was good, really good. The stormy, jagged past had drifted out the door. Their feelings were mutual.

Jean finished dicing the papaya and poked toothpicks into half of the cubes before setting the bowl aside and rinsing his hands. The sun had cleared the long horizon of ocean and risen into a long, black scud of clouds that had appeared from apparently nowhere. He peered at the clouds moving perceptibly in their direction. The back door banged shut, and Henry rounded the corner with Evie still straddling his hip.

"Those clouds don't look so good, do they?" the boy asked, seeing Jean at the window.

"No, they don't. Did you listen to the weather?"

"Not yet, but I can do that now. They've been talking about a tropical storm that could become a hurricane. It's supposed to go north, but those clouds look bad."

Henry was an adult in child's clothing. Jean laid a hand on his shoulder.

"We'll be just fine, buddy."

The worry on Henry's face morphed into a broad smile. He turned his head and gave Evie a playful bite on the neck. The child screeched.

Their brief conversation was over—their typical quick exchange of words between two non-talkers. Jean lifted the baby from Henry's arms. He kissed her chubby cheek, then turned to Lilly.

"Papaya's ready, boss."

Lilly tossed her head from her station at the toaster.

"I wish you wouldn't call me that."

"Why not, Mom, it's true," teased Henry, and ran out the kitchen door to the breezeway where single side band and VHF radios perched on a shelf above the desk that served as control central. The SSB crackled to life as a mechanical voice announced the area's weather. Lilly and Jean stood in the kitchen pretending to concentrate on breakfast preparations, their ears straining on the squawking weather report.

"A hurricane warning has been issued for the following locations . . ."

Jean saw Lilly's shoulders stiffen as the name of their island echoed against the soft peach walls. He crossed the kitchen, turned Lilly with a free hand, and tipped his head against hers.

"We'll be just fine," he assured her, and passed the gurgling baby to her before kissing both. "I'm going to find Ramón. He'll know more."

Lilly raised her hand to catch his sleeve, but he was already through the breezeway. A sudden pounding erupted in her chest. Jean's sudden exit accelerated her fear, and she raced after him past the radio still spewing news of impending disaster. Jean was already half-way down the hill to the road, his frenzied pace belying the calm demeanor she knew was meant for her assurance.

"Jean!" she called after him in a hollow croak.

He turned to wave and threw her a kiss. He felt her panic and forced it away. There would be time for comforting later. The radio forecast catastrophic wind speeds, heavy rain, coastal flooding—mayhem. They didn't have much time. His long strides picked up speed as the surrounding foliage swallowed the view of the house. He had to find Ramón—fast.

His feet scuffed through the rocky soil of the road on his way to town, a trip that typically took fifteen minutes. Today, he would make it in ten. His skin was buzzing with the sensation that only came from fear.

In the past, he had been immune to the sensation, when there was nothing to lose but his own life.

In the present, he had a family.

The spiraling vortex of the universe had drawn Lilly, Jean and the kids together in a most improbable location. He had first met Lilly, Henry, Amos and Sherri in the middle of nowhere southern California. He had been a crook. They were abandoned.

And now, they were his entire life. Nothing in existence was more important than Lilly and the kids. Then, of course there was Evie. A smile creased LaChance's face.

The exercise of reminiscing had done its duty, and occupied the frantic search for his friend Ramón. His sodden shirt clung in irregular pleats from his shoulders when he reached the edge of the village. He slowed to a walk and tried to ignore his drubbing chest. Up ahead, he spotted a group of men in a tight circle. Ramón was among them.

Chapter 2

Guy Santino flipped the keys in his hand, chose the silver one and slid it into the lock. The apartment didn't feel as empty after a day with his kids. Recently, time as he knew it had fast-forwarded on his children. Teenagers. Frightening, how quick life turned. The warm spot in his belly was filled with self-satisfaction, pride for his kids, pride for himself. Marta was sharing secrets with him formerly reserved for her mother. Don't tell Mom, she had pleaded. No way. He would carry that secret into his casket. He had once again become The Parent Who Held the Secrets. It was luxurious.

The tranquility lasted twenty, thirty minutes or so until the walls crowded around him once again. When he passed over the threshold, he crossed back into his own world, the one without homework, team sports on Friday night and new boyfriends. His mind meandered over a few chores he should be doing, then landed where it always did. With work. He popped the top of a beer and sat down with the remote, looking for a baseball game to inhabit his mind. Of course, it didn't work. Scattered among the pitches of Brian Barnes' left hand came thoughts of his most bothersome case. The one he couldn't shake.

Former Los Angeles Police Detective Guy Santino had failed in the Richard Prescott robbery case, now almost two years ago. None of the money had been recovered. The death of suspect Dewey Jensen remained unresolved. Jensen's former girlfriend, Lilly Parsons could not be connected to either the theft or the murder, though Santino was convinced she was somehow involved in both. Most importantly, and most maddening for Santino, the master-mind behind the Prescott heist—the professional—remained a mystery. Over one million dollars in cash had been stolen from the well-fortified Prescott house. No one but a professional could have accessed the house, disarmed the alarm system, found the hidden stash in a matter of minutes without leaving a smidgen of evidence. Santino and his partner, Jose had followed the trail of the blundering Jensen to an isolated desert location where he had reportedly lived. In the end, they found nothing but Jensen's corpse and a scatter of unidentifiable finger prints.

Lilly had known. She chose to enable the accomplice's escape from the Tucson airport, and accepted the possible consequences for herself and her children. But Santino had nothing on Lilly—only the fact that she had lived in the house at mile marker 256 in the desert where Dewey Jensen's corpse lay twisted on the parched earth. That was October.

Santino kept tabs on her afterward through the Tucson police, anticipating the reappearance of the ghost. Lilly and her kids resumed life at its regular pace, took no visitors, showed no sign of leaving or intending to leave. Then in May of the following year they had vanished—no forwarding address, no explanation to the kids' school, not even a courtesy phone call to the landlord. The house on Desert Way was left intact. There was food in the refrigerator, clothes in the closets, toys, cooking utensils, soap in the shower soap dish. When he got word, Santino hoped they had gone to visit her mother or a friend. But as weeks wore by and there was no sign, he was sure they were gone for good.

Santino had returned to the house in Tucson with Jose and turned it up-side-down, finding nothing but a vacated life. Santino laid odds that it was to join the ghost perp with the unidentifiable fingerprints.

The Los Angeles Police Commissioner rode his ass for weeks, making the remainder of his police career an infuriating game of hide-and-seek. Richard Prescott pulled every political chain to get the detective fired; dogging him in public, calling representatives and commissioners relentlessly until Santino had had enough. He submitted the reams of retirement paperwork that summer. By September, he was emancipated from the Los Angeles Police Department, with a pension and benefits sufficient for his lifestyle.

Years before he had traded his wife and kids for his career, an acrimonious, nagging mistake. Detective work defined him, and although he attempted standard retirement with its long lunches, golf, and afternoon drives, within a month he was clawing the walls. He enjoyed the free time with his kids, but his self-esteem required work. Santino opened a Private Investigator practice in November.

Cold cases came his way: missing persons, disgruntled wives seeking long-gone husbands, a few unsolved murders. The work was lucrative, and he discovered he could take as much as he needed to keep his brain engaged.

But the case involving Lilly Parsons plagued him, particularly at night when silence suffocated his sparse apartment. One of those troubled, sleepless nights he

Death of the Frenchman

unpacked his case file copies from basement storage at two a.m. The Richard Prescott case was unofficially reopened.

One huge clue that bugged Santino with a mosquito's persistence was the set of fingerprints from the house in the desert and Lilly's house in Tucson. Jose had called in a Tucson team to dust the house, and when the prints were analyzed, there they were. A textbook match. Whoever belonged to those fingerprints had master-minded the Prescott heist and likely killed Dewey Jensen.

Santino knew there was something unique about the owner of the prints. Their size; likely a man's. Their location indicated intimacy with the family, especially Lilly. It was improbable that a person with the skill to disarm Prescott's alarm system would have nothing on record. A career of crime required a specialized education, and mistakes came with that education. Yet there was nothing on record anywhere in the country. The ghost had vanished. Santino drew one conclusion. The ghost had to be a foreigner.

Despite his exile from law enforcement administration, Santino retained access to pivotal individuals who remained trusted friends. The connection provided access to forensic scientists who snuck Santino's occasional investigative requests through sophisticated analyses, a definite benefit to his new career. His best bet was Erin, a forensics administrator for the LAPD. She was a sweet red-head, about forty, with a luscious smile and a sailor's wit. They had crossed paths through the years, and became friends. Santino traded fingerprint analysis for dinner out, Erin's choice, which she collected one rainy May night at an Italian restaurant in the city.

They flirted at the table, and when the wine came, Santino poured both glasses and offered a toast.

"Salud," he said, hoisting the glass to the center of the duce.

"Salud Guy," she returned and tapped the side of his glass.

"Well, you were right, Detective," Erin began. She used the former title out of respect.

"I love to hear that," Santino answered. "About what?"

"Your perp is a foreigner."

"What? You found him?"

"I found him. It didn't take as long as I thought it would. And congratulations." She flipped a thirty-year-old mug shot onto the table facing Santino.

"You're looking for one of the most notorious professionals in France. His name is Jean LaChance."

A wave of electricity surged up the back of Santino's scalp as he stared into the eyes of his foe. The young face was long and hard—the eyes, even in the photo, made the hair on his arms stand at attention. The eyes of a jaguar stalking his prey.

The next half hour was occupied with Erin's report on LaChance. Dinner came as she detailed LaChance's history in Paris and beyond, the international palette of crime in which LaChance had prospered for years. Santino was mesmerized. He had known that the guy was a pro, but had had no idea of the extent of LaChance's involvement in some major unresolved cases. It seemed LaChance had slipped in and out of France, abetted by contractors, sneaking like a Ninja into wealthy villas and corporations, lifting only specific items with particular price tags. She concluded with the bank job that had triggered LaChance's flight from France two years earlier. When Erin finished, she set her glass down and folded her arms on the table.

"You've hit the lottery of thieves with Jean LaChance. Problem is that France hasn't heard a peep from him since that bank job. He has loads of aliases, according to Paris Police, so he could still be in France, but it's not likely."

Santino threw back the rest of his wine and poured another glass. Erin had done a good job. The news was both thrilling and terrifying. Santino had a face and profile to fit the fingerprints. The terrifying part was LaChance's skill level, no doubt exceeding his own. It was little wonder he had not been able to catch the man. He replayed the scene in the desert two years before when they had arrived at Lilly's house too eagerly, giving the French thief ample warning and a chance to escape. They hadn't known anyone was there. Dewey's corpse out back of the house had stalled them just long enough for LaChance to slip away, with perhaps up to an hour lead time. Even in the remote stretches of the California desert, it was more than enough.

The exhilaration of the moment brought a shudder. Imagine. Guy Santino on the tail of one of the most wanted men in France.

He reached over and grabbed Erin's hand and kissed it, checking to see her reaction. Santino had been flirting with Erin for years, but during his time as a detective, he was reluctant to act on it. Could be it was time.

"Is this foreplay?" Erin asked.

"Do you want it to be?"

"You bastard. Treat me right or I'll leave right now." She was smiling.

"This is big, Erin. I knew two years ago this guy was a pro just from how easily he accessed the house—how clean it was. The other guy with him, Dewey Jensen was a moron—his prints were everywhere. But not one from Mr. LaChance. He also showed us our asses when we finally caught up to him. Got out clean right from under our noses. I knew he was good. No wonder."

Santino's voice drifted off. His expression sobered.

"What's wrong?" Erin asked.

"Hmm?"

"Something wrong?"

"I don't know. Man, he might've spared our lives. Somebody like that, waiting. We could all be dead by now."

"Oh, come on. He was running from you," Erin said.

"I know, I know. But I'll bet he knows what I look like. Guys like that . . . guys like that don't miss."

"Well, you're lucky then, think about it that way."

"Yeah, lucky. Nobody's heard a word from him or the woman in a long time. The following May, Lilly and her kids disappeared. Just disappeared. Two years ago this month."

"Do you think they met up with him?"

Santino looked up.

"I don't know. What do you think?"

Chapter 3

Santino exited the highway at Coachella. Lilly's mother Evelyn Murray was still alive, living in the same trailer park—bitter, dispossessed, angry, vile. Santino shook his head when he recalled how quickly she had given up information about her only child, greedy for a finder's fee. But there was still a chance that she knew where Lilly had landed.

In the more than two years since he had last taken the same exit, little had changed of the town where Evelyn resided. The day was painfully hot from the punishing sun and lack of rain that defined the weather of southern California desert. Recalling his meeting with the hag of a woman, he almost hoped she wasn't home, but he knew she would be. Evelyn Murray was the type of woman who would never venture far from her tumble-down trailer, in the most affordable place she could find with habitable weather. She reminded him of a sloth—one who was too lazy to even clean herself, or make anything of her life—angry at the world for what it had made her, unable to change or improve in any way, socially ungrateful; revolting.

Though the woman was repulsive, for some weird reason, Santino could remember where she lived. Even revulsion created memories, and Evelyn Murray was certainly memorable. The car growled along the crumbling pavement through residential neighborhoods that depreciated with every block. Santino's neck grew tighter as the distance to the trailer narrowed.

A newish Cadillac was parked outside the single-wide dump at a slight angle, and at first Santino thought it meant she had moved. There hadn't been a car two years ago. Evelyn Murray looked like she couldn't afford a used bicycle.

As soon as he opened his car door, he was accosted by the blast of heat accompanied by a deafening volume of day-time TV from the trailer.

No. She's still here.

He leaned over the rickety aluminum steps and rapped on the door.

"Who is it?" a raspy voice demanded over the blasting court drama.

"It's Guy Santino."

"Who?"

The TV volume cut abruptly. The bang of the metal door was followed by a rolling billow of cigarette smoke steeped with cheap hair spray. A slightly older version of Evelyn Murray stood framed in the door, ever-present cigarette pinched between her fingers, same scowl stamped across her swollen face. Despite this, she looked better than she had the last time. The formerly greasy, uncombed hair was dyed and coiffed. She was wearing new clothes.

"Oh, it's you," Evelyn snarled and fell into a coughing fit. Her personality had not changed along with her hair. She recovered from her fit.

"What do you want now?" she demanded.

"I'm just following up on old cases, Mrs. Murray. I know it's been some time since I've seen you, and I want to thank you again for the information on your daughter, Lilly."

"Lillian? Where is she?"

"Well, that's just the thing. We don't know. I found her two years ago when we were looking for her last boyfriend, Dewey Jensen."

"Where was she then?" Evelyn asked.

"She was in Tucson."

Santino caught the split-second flicker of light in Evelyn's eyes, but it died just as quickly. A brief, yet unmistakable "something to hide" response. Two years ago, the only thing that had interested her was the prospect of reward money for information on Lilly's whereabouts.

"So . . . she still there?" Evelyn asked in a sly growl.

"No, no, she's not there. She left Tucson about a year and a half ago. Didn't you know?"

"Lillian and I are not close," the woman said. "She can't be bothered with me."

"So you don't happen to know where she is now?"

"What's in it for me?" the woman asked, and paused for a second to allow Santino a chance to respond, which he ignored. "I didn't hear from you after our conversation, or did I?"

Odd question. There was more to her comment than the crusty exchange divulged. Santino was sure she knew something.

"No, you didn't hear from me, Mrs. Murray. There was no news to report. We found Lilly, but we never recovered anything from the robbery committed by her

Death of the Frenchman

boyfriend. We know she wasn't directly involved in the crime." He paused, then added, "Police departments don't typically issue rewards for information."

Evelyn leaned heavily against the aluminum door jamb, and the entire trailer shifted in response.

"Well, I got nothin' to tell you, Detective. I ain't seen or heard from her."

"Okay, then, thank you, Mrs. Murray. If you hear anything at all, please give me a call."

He handed her his card. She glanced at it quickly.

"Oh, you're private dick now, huh?"

"Yes, ma'am. I retired from the force a while ago."

"Yeah, well, I want nothin' to do with the police or any private dick."

"Okay then, thank you," Santino said and turned toward his car. "Oh, by the way, nice car."

"Yeah, I got lucky since I saw you last."

Evelyn Murray slammed the light door, shaking the length of the aluminum. Santino jumped in his car and headed toward the highway.

Got lucky, he thought. What were the odds? Lilly had known about the stolen money. She had fessed up when they questioned her. Was it possible that Evelyn Murray had received some of that money? *I didn't hear from you after our conversation, or did I?* She had tripped a bit with the bizarre question. She had also offered information in exchange for a reward two years ago. A dysfunctional family, to be sure, but even dysfunctional families shared their spoils.

When Santino reached the highway, he looked right toward L.A., then left in the direction of Tucson.

"What the hell," he said out loud, and took a left.

Chapter 4

By mid-morning news of the storm had spread to every shore of the island. Tropical storm Stephanie (coined by the United States National Weather Service) was now a hurricane, sucking power from balmy Caribbean waters. Overnight, it had taken a left toward the northern shore of Venezuela and all the islands in-between. All Caribbean residents had been keeping one eye on the growth of the storm for some time, even before it was strong enough to warrant a name. Residents of the island were accustomed to the typical track of hurricanes that charged up through the middle of the Caribbean, across Cuba or Jamaica and then on to terrorize the East Coast or Gulf States of the U.S. Rarely did storms come this way, so the island lived in relative security during the annual June through November hurricane season.

Though some newer houses were "hurricane proof," most island dwellings were far too old to meet construction codes. Some were just huts. Phone lines strung on tall leaning posts in remote rural areas were easily reattached after high winds by anyone with a hammer and some nails. Ninety percent of the residents, rich and poor alike, had built cisterns of every design to catch rain water. Some were nothing more than a barrel hooked to a make-shift plumbing system, while new models were poured cement structures the size of semi-tractors that held thousands of gallons.

Jean and Lilly's guest house had a twenty-year-old, sixty-thousand gallon cistern, generally adequate for average capacity. Small notices in the bathrooms and kitchens encouraged guests to conserve water, but water conservation in general was common place, and considerate customers generally complied. A new cistern for the property was in the plans to supplement the original one, which was leaking up to several gallons of water a day. Ramón had worked on it several times, but had failed to find the leak. It was a matter of constant frustration, but today, LaChance's problem was just the opposite.

He found Ramón near the post office talking with some of the village men. The conversation was intense and they ignored his arrival. Jean's moderate understanding of the brisk Spanish chatter was clarified by the abnormally edgy manner of island-speak. He stood for a time on the margin of the circle and listened. Details were lost, but he knew for certain what was being discussed. The hurricane had turned their way and would arrive by nightfall.

After the men dispersed, Ramón turned to Jean.

"This hurricane is coming, you know," Ramón said. Worry was hard on his face.

"Yes, I gathered that. Is it too late for the guests to get out?"

"How many do you have?" Ramón asked.

"There are ten guests, and we are six," Jean answered.

"Call the airport. I would imagine all the flights are booked by now. All the visitors will be trying to leave."

"I was thinking we should empty the cistern. It's our only chance."

"Yes, my friend, yes, and do it now. I have to go to my home and then help a friend, but I will come by later to check on you. Please begin very soon. It will take a while."

The two men locked forearms and Jean turned toward home. Though he was unaccustomed to hurrying, he ran all the way back to the house. His pulse was racing and sweat streamed down inside his shirt. Danger was a familiar foe, but he had always faced it alone. Now there were five loved ones and ten guests. He was terrified.

Lilly took one look at his face and gasped. Henry stood up from his breakfast plate so fast the chair toppled to the floor.

"We have to empty the cistern, Henry," he said, looking all the while at Lilly. "Come on."

"Jean!" Lilly cried after him.

He turned, walked over and hugged her.

"Don't worry, Lilly, just do as I say. This hurricane is coming and we have only until nightfall to prepare. After Henry and I get back, we'll discuss what to do."

"But Jean . . ."

"Lilly!" he barked. She jumped.

He softened his tone. "Call the airport right now and ask whether we can book any of our guests today. I'll be back soon."

Death of the Frenchman

Lilly clamped her mouth shut and watched them leave. Tears erupted from her eyes. She didn't mind the way he had snapped at her. Men in her past had been much worse. But Jean was not reactive. The outburst exposed fear. If Jean was afraid, she was petrified. She leaned her forehead against baby Evie and cried.

Henry ran to all the guest rooms one by one, greeting the guests, and began by urging them and finally showing them how to open all the spigots in their bathrooms to empty the cistern as quickly as possible. Confusion escalated into confrontation and eventually Henry gave up and went to find Jean. LaChance was straining with a gigantic wrench, attempting to free an outside petcock on the cistern.

The Japanese woman was standing at her door with a towel wrapped tight on her head.

"Mr. LaPorte! Why this boy tell us to open the water? We have finish shower."

Jean was starting to explain when two of the other guests appeared outside their doors with the same question. He apologized for the confusion, then began to explain in a calm, quiet tone. When he reached the word "hurricane," the looks on the guests' faces foreshadowed the panic he expected.

"Please, please," he said gesturing with both hands. "Please, just open all the taps. We have to empty the cistern. It is the only safe place for us to go. Please stay close at hand. I will come to get you soon."

The German man spoke up.

"Mr. LaPorte, is it possible to leave the island?"

"We are looking into that now, sir," Jean answered. "I will speak with you all soon. Please open all the taps."

Jean's strides were so long Henry had to run to keep up with him.

"Jean?"

The man looked down at the boy he loved. Henry's eyes were paralyzed with worry. It was time to be a father.

Jean stopped and knelt down, putting his face on the same level as Henry's, suddenly noticing how much the boy had grown. He reached up and grasped both shoulders.

"Wow, you're getting tall," Jean said. Henry smiled.

"Listen, we have to hurry and prepare for the storm. We'll go inside the cistern, and we'll be fine. I need you right now because your mother is very frightened, the guests are frightened, and you must be brave so you can help me. Can you do that?"

Henry nodded, wiping his eyes with the back of his hand.

"When you left California, I came and found you, remember?"
Henry nodded again.
"I'll never leave you, buddy. I'll always be here, okay?"
The boy smiled.
"Okay, Dad."
Jean laughed and hugged Henry hard, then was instantly serious.

The darkened sky fashioned eerie white points of light. Swirling wind coaxed the palm trees into spooky patterns, forewarning the tempest closing in from the east.

Jean found Lilly changing the baby. He turned her around and saw that she'd been crying.

"Lilly, Lilly, Lilly, mon cheri." He drew her by her hands over to the side of the bed and sat her down. Tears fell now with comfort close at hand, and Jean caressed the side of her face.

"Lilly, there is a big hurricane coming. We need to get ready."
She nodded rapidly.
"Did you call the airport?"
"Yes, there are no flights out."
"Prepare food, something we can eat without cooking. Food and water. We'll need blankets, some pillows, flashlights, buckets." The calm voice detailed a long list of supplies they would need for a night of bedlam. As he went on, she relaxed and listened, intent on his eyes and his smooth, commanding voice. When he finished, he looked at her. Her small face was cradled in his palms.

"We're going to be just fine, Lilly. We've been through worse than this."
"Alright, you're right," she said.
"Do you think I would let anything happen to you? To any of you?"
"No."
"Okay then."

He took a bit more time and held Lilly close on the edge of the bed. He kissed her face and hands and murmured softly in French. Little Evie, forgotten on the changing table, squealed in protest and broke the spell.

They had five hours before the arrival of the storm.

Chapter 5

The four hour drive to Tucson provided valuable thinking time. During the Richard Prescott/Lilly Parsons case, Santino had spent too much time chasing them and not enough getting to know them. The mistake might have cost him the case, and now they were long gone. Was this obsession driven by guilt? Guilt or insecurity, he wasn't sure which. Probably both. The case nagged him, like a cranky wife. Perhaps it was that "gut instinct" they talked about. Santino chuckled out loud.

Rewinding the case in his mind was a tantalizing game, and he did it deliberately, and often. But now the odds had changed. They were in his favor. His ghost had a face and a name.

Jean LaChance.

Even the name sounded risky, sinister. The face was distinctive. People might remember him.

But who? Who would be able to identify him? Lilly's neighbors? Her landlord? Would it mean anything if he could be identified? It was the context that mattered. LaChance had spent time with Lilly and the kids. The trail was as cold as Alaskan February. What Santino needed was information about the money. The Frenchman was gone, had been gone for almost two years. Had he taken the money with him? Unlikely, that amount of cash. So, if he couldn't take it, where would he hide it?

Santino had considered banks. It was a logical deduction. Visiting banks would have done no good without a face. But now he had a face. A face might give him a name if LaChance had used an alias. A name might produce a trail. The Prescott robbery had involved over one million dollars in cash, an amount which was easy to move given plenty of time. LaChance had not had much time with Santino on his tail. From the day of the crime to LaChance's departure from Tucson, less than three weeks had elapsed. Legitimate deposits would have to be small to avoid raising flags and would have taken too long.

A guy like LaChance would have done something else. Like hide the money somewhere, wait for the heat to cool down, then come back and collect it. It could be buried so far out in the desert that no one would ever be able to find it, or it could be hidden in a large urban setting right under everyone's noses. Whatever it was, it would be something simple. That's what LaChance would do, Santino thought. LaChance was also from the city. He would go where he was comfortable, rather than out to an unfamiliar wild environment. Santino decided to start with the banks.

Reopening the case brought him new life. His heart thumped in his chest, and he felt vigorous, alive. Just the possibility. The possibility of discovering what he—what they had done with the money—was enough to expunge the failure of having blown the case.

He glanced over to the passenger's seat where Jean LaChance's twenty-something-year-old face stared up at the headliner. He lifted the photo and placed it on the steering wheel. The eyes were distant, deep, secret. The face was strong and determined. This was the face of a warrior, a formidable rival. Santino had to be careful. LaChance was the kind of man who was capable of anything, particularly when cornered. The mug shot had been taken following his one arrest for burglary—and it wasn't LaChance's slip that got him caught. One of his competitors had dropped a dime during the crime, Erin had said. His capture was unavoidable, but that was the only time, and he wasn't locked up for long. The Paris Police had not had the pleasure of Jean LaChance's company since then. Santino wondered what might have happened to the rat, and shivered.

LaChance was now close to fifty years old, and Santino didn't doubt his skills had sharpened. He gazed at the photo and tried to age the face in his mind. Had he seen him at the airport? Santino couldn't be sure. But he wouldn't miss again.

The Tucson Police Department was helpful. Santino re-connected with the sergeant who had accompanied him to the airport when LaChance had slipped from them, but he didn't remember the Frenchman's face, either.

There were two hundred thirty eight banks including branches in the greater Tucson area. Within the day, the LaChance mug shot would be circulated, and bank staffs would be briefed. Bank records would be searched for any transaction conducted under the name Jean LaChance, though it was impossible he would have used his real name. Tellers and officers would be tasked with recalling a face from two years before, during a transaction that may have lasted less than minutes.

Death of the Frenchman

They would be looking for a French man, perhaps with an accent, which would make the search easier but not easy. It would take several days, perhaps a week, and Santino decided to stay in the area, just in case.

He left the Department headquarters and found himself driving to Lilly's former residence on Desert Way, the last place he had seen her. LaChance had been in that house.

Curtains in the windows and a car in the driveway indicated current tenants. Santino knocked on the door and spoke to a young woman holding a baby. No, she didn't know anything about the former tenants, in fact, had only been living there five months. No, they hadn't found anything unusual in the house, but he was welcome to search, because she had nothing to hide. Santino politely declined, aware that any possible evidence would have been destroyed months ago.

He excused himself and turned to go, then thought of a question that might lead to some answers.

"Excuse me, Miss? Just one more question, if you don't mind. Do you have other children?"

"Yes, I do, one son. He's in school."

"Is it close?"

"Yes, it's just down the main street four blocks and one block to the left. It's really convenient."

"Good, thank you. Thank you very much."

Santino found the school easily and asked directions to the office. The women in the office were surprisingly forthcoming with information about the family and remembered the children well. They remembered Lilly as a sweet woman who loved her children and followed their education closely. She attended Parent-Teacher conferences, right up to their sudden departure.

"It was strange, Investigator," the head secretary said.

"What was strange?"

"The kids were still in school until the middle of May. One day, they simply didn't show up, and never came back. The Truant Officer checked on it, but they had left their place of residence. There was no word after that. We figured that they had gone back to join family before the baby came."

"The baby?" Santino asked.

"Yes, Lilly Parsons was pregnant, quite pregnant, maybe six or seven months. We chatted about the baby one time when Ms. Parsons came to pay a fee. She was a little evasive about the father, and we never saw a man. We thought maybe the father was not with them, and she didn't share any information. She was very nice.

She loved her children very much. What a sweet family. I felt sorry for them. It seemed they were on their own."

"Yes, I guess they were."

"So, you have no idea where they are now?"

"No, ma'am, no idea."

"What a shame. Those kids were special. Very well-behaved. Very respectful. Their mother had done a good job. I just hope they're safe."

"I'm sure they are."

Santino excused himself from the office, thankful for the office busy-body who stuck her nose where it didn't belong. He sat in his car for a while thinking about the new information and his next move.

The baby. LaChance's child? The math worked out perfectly. LaChance had been with them in October, and an older, knowledgeable woman had put her at six or seven months pregnant in May.

There was the motive. If LaChance and Lilly had had an affair, then maybe Dewey Jensen's murder was a crime of passion. If Lilly was not in contact with her mother, perhaps she had gone somewhere to join LaChance, the father of her child. The already intriguing case was getting better with every snippet of new information. Although he was wound up and ready for more action, some food and a good night's sleep would be the smart thing. He started the car and went on a hunt for a hotel.

Chapter 6

Building wind gusts from the southeast drove the angry clouds. The typically blue-green waves, now black with terror, raced far up the beach to drag the white sand back out to the depths of the sea. Rain fell in drenching sheets that puddled on the high ground until the sheer volume spilled over, seeking its lowest point. Lilly struggled with a load of supplies up the slope to the cistern cap, where she passed it through to outstretched hands.

Everyone had waited until the last minute to climb into the monstrous square cement cistern that still held over two feet of water. Lilly glanced back toward the house, where Jean was heaving a large plastic box up the hill. When he reached the top, Lilly helped him squeeze the box through to the guests who placed it on the floor of the cistern and piled the wet supplies on top. The howling wind stole Jean's shout to the children huddled in the house doorway, but they had been waiting for his call and saw the wave of his arm. They raced up the hill hand-in-hand and Jean passed them through one by one before he and Lilly climbed into the hole. The cap slammed shut, and the sound of the wind dropped to a hush while the others held flashlights for Jean as he grunted against the tight lever rusty from infrequent use. Over the distant racket, heavy breathing was the only sound in the subterranean tomb-turned-refuge. Dancing flashlight beams illuminated the wild eyes of the trapped inhabitants, as each one rode an emotional roller coaster of safety followed by panic. They were out of the hurricane, but shelter could become doom. A landslide would seal them where life-giving air could never reach.

Jean crawled down the ladder into the knee-high water and took baby Evie from the American woman named Sue. The woman was crying, and he placed a hand on her arm.

"I'm so sorry this has happened to you during your stay here," he said to everyone in the cistern. "Let's hope for the best. The water will continue to drain, and I've sealed the intake, so we should be fine."

"What about air?" asked a male voice.

"I know several of the local residents who have been through this. It's a large cistern, and we should be okay for hours, but we might have to open the cap if we have trouble breathing."

"What if we can't get the cap closed again?" the same voice asked.

"We'll get it closed." Jean's comment ran over the question. "The hurricane may last all night, so it's possible that we will have to open it more than once, but we'll get it closed."

Silence dropped over the tight cement walls. He wanted to feel the confidence his voice conveyed. He glanced around in the shadows and found Lilly. She was shivering.

"Are you cold, my love? There are blankets in the bags. Please, if anyone is cold, we have blankets and extra clothes."

They had been instructed to dress in layers. At present, they all were cold from standing in the water, but as time wore on, the cement cistern could grow warm with the combined body heat of sixteen people. They were forced to stand for the time being, but as the last of the water drained from the tank, they would be able to sit or lie down on the floor.

"Daddy, I'm scared," Sherri whimpered. Jean handed the baby to Lilly and knelt down to lift Sherri onto his shoulders, where she would be spared from the cold water which reached to her waist. Amos and Henry huddled together in one corner.

The seconds ticked by as the refugees grew accustomed to the creepy chamber. They began exchanging names and information amongst the beams of light bouncing about in the dark. Night vision came mercifully. After one hour, someone announced the time, and groans echoed against the walls. A consensus was reached to call out the time on the hour, so they could track the oxygen level and the passage of the night.

From inside the safety of their sanctuary, they could hear the howling wind gusts build to a groan and then, a gruesome screech. Ear-splitting crashes brought cries and frantic questions as Stephanie began to dismantle the island's infrastructure. Downed trees? Pieces of buildings? Systematic checks were taken of all sixteen people. The panic was steady, pervasive. Terror erased the fatigue they should have felt from standing and waiting endlessly in one place.

Death of the Frenchman

By hour two, Sherri and Evie had fallen asleep in their parents' arms. The water had retreated to a depth of six inches, but the children could not yet be lowered to the floor. The baby's head bobbed on Lilly's arm. Evie was already more than twenty pounds, and none of them could hold her for long. One man offered to take Sherri, but Jean declined. Henry and Amos huddled together in a blanket and finally relented their weary bodies to the cement floor, where they sat sleeping against the wall, the corners of the blanket floating around their legs like seaweed.

Another hour crawled by, and the air in the cistern grew heavy. A vote was taken to open the cap for fresh air, and the men formulated a plan. Jean woke Sherri and lowered the whining child to the floor, then climbed the ladder to the underside of the cap. The men below supported his legs. The women held flashlights. On the count of three, he released the lever. The split second he pushed the lid open a crack, a violent gust ripped the handle out of his hand, wrenching his shoulder badly and crashing the cap back on its hinges.

Screaming horror invaded their shelter. Chocolate-colored water poured in a torrent down into the mouth of the cistern, covering Jean with sludge. Screeches of every note in the scale erupted from the human captives, and merged with the anger of the storm. The men clutched Jean's legs and howled at the raging wind. Jean crept farther up the ladder, his body pinned by the force of the wind against one side of the hole. He found the handle with his good arm. The open cap barely moved. He jerked the handle again and again without success. Opaque water splattered the heads and bodies of the panicky tourists. Jean dropped down from the ladder and screamed over the tempest.

"Someone else try!" He fell back into the cistern, gripping his shoulder with his good arm.

They chose the largest of the men, Hans the German, who crawled carefully up the ladder for a turn at the cap, with no luck. Horror swelled in the cement tomb as the level of the water, mixed with mud was rising along the walls. The German retreated.

"I can't budge it!" he shouted.

"Let me try once more!" Jean ordered, and climbed the ladder again. "Let's count to three—then pull me down!"

LaChance listened for the rhythm of the heavy gusts. He forced his mind to calm and breathed strength into his body. Once he determined some regularity in the bursts, he counted loudly to three and threw all of his remaining strength into the handle. The cap slammed shut, and he secured the lever. He collapsed onto the floor in agony.

Sounds of gasping filled the cistern. Lilly knelt down in the muck beside Jean. "Are you alright?"

Tears ran down his expressionless face, making clear tracks through the mud. "I think so. Yes, I'll be alright."

Morbid worry was stamped on the faces of the men standing around him. Jean was the strongest man in the cistern. With him injured, they would have to wait as long as possible to open the cap for more air.

"What's the time?" asked the Japanese man.

"It's nine thirty," one woman answered.

"So we've been in here for four and a half hours, right?"

Murmurs of agreement bounced off the walls.

"In another four hours, the wind should have died a little," Jean said from his place on the floor. "Either way, we can't worry about that now." He turned to Lilly, who had started to massage his injured shoulder. He pushed her away. "Are the kids okay?"

"Yes, they're fine, honey," she answered. She smoothed his hair and caressed his forehead. "We're going to be just fine, I know."

"Yes, we will," Jean answered. "Je t'aime, mon cheri."

"I love you too, Jean."

A sudden deafening crash above shook the cistern violently. A chorus of screams followed.

"What was that?" someone asked.

"Sounds like something landed on top of us."

A mournful lull crept through the cement crypt, and quiet sounds of sniffing were heard over the shrieks above.

"What if we can't get out?" another voice whispered.

"We can't worry about that now," Jean ordered. "We'll get out. Many people know we're down here."

No one said a word, but all minds were on the same wavelength. What if no one else was alive? What if rescue took too long and the oxygen ran out? Nightmarish visions raced through their imaginations; locals prying the cistern open to find only corpses below.

Jean was right. They simply had to wait.

Each minute in the cistern was slow, steady torture. Time is strange, thought LaChance. Depending on the emotion of the situation, it flew or dragged at turns. This night would be endless. He leaned his head back against the cement wall and put himself through an exercise he had learned long ago. Back then, he used the mind game to calm himself before a risky job, where he needed all of his wits. But it was also effective in controlling panic. The idea was to summon images of happiness or success. He closed his eyes, and his vision turned a dull shade of white. His practiced mind began to expunge the pain, the shrieking wind, the people standing against the cement walls. The slow passage of time triggered memories of the four days at the house in the desert two years before. Those days spent waiting for Dewey Jensen. Those four days. Four short days had irreversibly altered LaChance's life. Thank God for that time. It had given them the chance to fall in love.

Jean LaChance was now legally Pierre LaPorte, and the island natives knew him as "Mr. Pierre." Passport, deeds, legal documents all bore the name Pierre LaPorte. Lilly found it impossible to adopt the name that legitimized his existence, and would forever call him Jean. Days and weeks swept by in a maze of chores and tasks necessary to get their business up and running. They were safe. They were living a new life.

Two months after their arrival on the island, Lilly had given birth to Constance Evelyn LaPorte, named for both Jean's and Lilly's mothers, conceived in the little house in the California desert. From the beginning, Lilly had called the baby Evie, and it stuck, even for Jean, who idolized his long-dead mother whom he scarcely remembered. Lilly never provided an explanation for her choice of the child's pet name. Evie was Evie. The whole family called her that, though sometimes on rare sleepless nights, Jean would wake and rock his only natural child on the bungalow veranda and whisper the name "Constance" in her ear. Their secret gave him comfort and a connection with his former life, now a simple wisp of memory.

LaChance reached over Lilly's shoulder and touched Evie's blond fuzzy hair with just the tips of his fingers. Lilly stirred awake, saw the gesture and stretched up to kiss him. She was stiff with the cold of the cistern, the fright of interment.

An endless night-long vigil crept by in increments. Conversation was low and meaningful. Voices spoke of families; children and grandchildren, parents and siblings. Flashlight batteries died and were replenished. They opened and ate cold canned stew, shared fresh fruit and sections of sandwiches Lilly had prepared. A small porta-potti provided relief behind a blanket held high to preserve dignity.

After what seemed like days, someone noticed that the wind was becoming less frightening, harder to hear.

Hourly times were called out with growing emotion through the midnight hours of Stephanie's bedlam. Prayers were chanted in animated foreign whispers.

Familiar Bible passages were inserted into the meager conversation. Slowly, imperceptibly, again the air grew stiff and thick.

"Let's try to open the cap again," Hans said. Consensus echoed through the cistern. He volunteered. At the top, he loosed the lever, and gripped the handle tightly, expecting a jerk. Nothing happened. He hesitantly applied pressure. The cap refused to budge.

"Oh, no!" one woman cried. "We're trapped! We'll suffocate in here!"

"Let's calm down," Jean ordered. "We'll use more oxygen and we won't do ourselves any good. Hans," he said to the man at the top of the ladder. "Climb up higher and put your shoulder against the cap. Guys, let's get under and help him."

All the men jostled for a spot at the foot of the ladder as Hans climbed as high as he could and braced his shoulder and neck on the bottom of the cap. They counted to three, and heaved their weight against the lid. Nothing moved.

"Again," Jean said. They counted to three, and the stubborn cap lifted a few inches. Fresh air mixed with muddy water streamed into the hole, but the water slowed to drips after ten seconds. They strained their ears to the world outside. The wind was strong, but no longer terrifying. The time was three thirty in the morning, and daylight was a couple of hours away.

They all agreed to leave the cap cracked a bit to allow fresh air to circulate. Despite the heavy weight on the roof of the cistern, the frantic emotion had settled, and sporadic laughter punctuated the darkness. Jean and Lilly huddled in one corner. Lilly was nodding off. Henry, Amos and Sherri were collapsed across the laps of both adults, asleep only because their little brains had mercifully shut down.

LaChance's shoulder screamed with pain. It felt as if fire had invaded his body. The lurch of the cap thrown by the powerful wind had strained tendons, and though Lilly administered dose after dose of any pain killer she could find in the blackness, it didn't touch the misery. Jean was not a complainer, but every movement left him wincing. She knew she had to watch him closely to assess his condition.

The last hour of imprisonment was eternal, as the inhabitants of the cistern waited for daylight. Intermittent conversation was indiscernible. Last stretch fatigue had taken over. One by one, they retired to the slimy floor, and were falling asleep. Even LaChance was nodding off for several minutes at a time.

"Mommy, the sun!"

Sherri's reveille jolted the adults awake. They stared at the sliver of dusky light peeking under the bottom of the cap. With most of them asleep during the last hour, little notice had been given to the wind levels. Their focus on the gap of light, the survivors realized that the wind had abated, that sunlight was breaking through. Jean and Lilly lifted the kids off their laps and stood. Their filthy clothes clung to them like tree bark. Lilly peeled Jean's shirt sleeve up and gasped when she saw his shoulder was a swollen mass of vivid colors.

"Let's see if we can lift the cap," he said.

The men gathered at the foot of the ladder and sent up Hans. The strain turned his face cherry red, but the cap refused to budge. Jean peered through the gap and recognized the green tiles against the cistern top. It was the roof of his house. Hans dug his fingers through the mud and widened the gap slightly, but it was clear that they would not release themselves from their overnight prison cell.

So they waited.

With the aid of daylight, Lilly dove into the packets of supplies to come up with anything to eat. The sixteen munched on muffins and fruit and engaged in small talk; the impending rescue, a shower, a hot cup of tea. After "breakfast," Lilly produced a bottle of water and some face cloths that she passed to the guests and used to bathe the children, who were exhausted into silence. Sherri whimpered quietly. Baby Evie, having been hard-wired with her father's tough character, slept through the mayhem on her mother's shoulder.

"Listen!" a voice cried.

The cement vault fell silent. From above, faint voices could be heard in the distance. Without a prompt, all the inhabitants of the cistern began screaming. Even at the end of their energy, they mustered an ensemble loud enough to be heard above the retreating wind through a crack inches wide, across the wrecked landscape to the ears of fellow survivors spending their first minutes of liberty looking for neighbors and friends.

Within seconds, voices babbling rapid Spanish surrounded the gap above their heads. The whine of chainsaws, the thunk of hatchets, and the wheezing of carpenter saws joined the prisoners' chorus as a small army of locals descended on the cistern. The cap snapped back on its hinges and hands reached through to grab hands, and pulled the shaken victims from their filthy refuge.

Jean was last out of the hole. Ramón stood outside, his clothes streaked with mud.

"Mi amigo," Ramón said, clapping his hands on Jean's back.

Jean stood for a second clasping the hands of his savior. He lifted his eyes with hesitation, and took in the scene around him.

Swirling wind gusts buffeted the yard where the cistern had held its ground. The immediate area was unrecognizable. Wreckage littered the surrounding ground so thickly, no vegetation was visible. There had once been a thick privacy screen of trees lining the outskirts of the property. Only ghostly sticks remained. Their guest house stood on a high point; the porch overlooking the sleepy village. Now the remains of what had once been the village could be seen clearly from where Jean was standing. The footprint of the house was a massive pile of splinters, with twisted pieces of metal that had once been appliances thrown here and there. The once neat guest house property might as well have been a landfill.

Jean stumbled helplessly in a circle, taking in the devastation that Stephanie had brought to their paradise in the course of one night. The pain was hidden behind his eyes, but tears ran down his cheeks. His circle ended at the point it had started, the face of his good friend, Ramón.

"You are alright, yes?" Ramón said quietly.

"Yes, yes, we are all fine."

Lilly was standing off to the side holding the baby and now came to embrace their rescuer. Ramón had grown up on this island. It was a utopia that cradled its inhabitants and fed them with its bounty. But when the sea stood up, it claimed everything. Ramón understood this. He had seen it before. For Lilly and Jean, the shock following the nightmare of Hurricane Stephanie tipped the scales. Lilly started to cry.

Jean pulled the sobbing woman into his arms and held her so long that Ramón finally felt the need to intervene.

"Please, please come with us. All of you," he gestured to the tourists. "Please, you need food and rest. Please come."

Chapter 7

Henry peeled around the corner of a cement structure that was the sole surviving building on the island's windward shore. A bag of fresh coconuts swung from his hand; a precious find following a storm as vicious as Stephanie. His mother would be proud. He trotted down the main street of the village which was slowly coming back to life by the hands of its residents. The town had been nearly erased in the wake of the hurricane. As he neared the tent that had become their temporary home, he whistled for his brother.

"Amos! Come help me open these coconuts."

The tent flap flipped back and Lilly's grin emerged.

"Coconuts! You smart boy. Amos, go and help Henry."

Her good boy Henry. It had only been a week, and she was already sick of canned food. It stirred memories of the house in the desert where Dewey Jensen had abandoned them, where the food had run so scarce that Henry, then age ten, became a gopher hunter, and fed the family for weeks. How life had changed in such a short time. She broke from her mind journey back to the task at hand, washing clothes for five people and a baby in a tub, complete with washboard.

Yes, life certainly had changed.

She glanced over her shoulder to her sleeping husband. For one week he had done little but sleep. Angry black-purple marks on his shoulder were starting to fade, but a doctor confirmed the tendons had sustained damage, and might never be the same.

Fucking storm. Why did this have to happen? Life had been so good. In the space of two years, she had gone from abandonment and poverty to giddy contentment: the birth of her fourth child, her love child, fathered by the man she treasured more than life. A leisurely idyllic existence on a tropical island, a life that had been smashed overnight by a maverick phenomenon of nature.

The first two days were spent just recovering from shock, feeding the children and attending to their needs. Were the kids scarred for life? Should they leave this island? Jean had been in horrible pain and said very little. He had withdrawn into his invisible inner sanctum and slept long hours, his back to the center of the tent, immovable, nursing his remaining pride. Lilly was worried; worried about her kids, her husband, her life. With Jean inaccessible at present, time became an agonizing pause until his strength returned.

She finished the wash and lugged it outside to the rigged clothesline. Stripped palm trees stood like ribbed telephone poles for hundreds of yards along the street. In time, the trees would recover completely. They had evolved over millennia to survive storms that would destroy northern trees. They simply sacrificed their leaves and fruit, both of which grew back without a problem in a short amount of time. Would they recover as well? Lilly sighed and turned toward the tent.

Jean was standing just inside the flap watching her. He beckoned her and when she approached, wrapped her in a warm hug, rocking back and forth. When he finally let go, she tipped her face back to see his smile.

"Well, hello," she said. "Who are you?"

Jean chuckled and hugged her again.

"I'm so sorry, Lilly. I've been in terrible pain, and losing . . . losing everything . . ."

He didn't finish the sentence. Failure was an alien concept; failure with the added weight of a wife and four children. She kissed his chin gently.

"Now that you're back, we'll be fine. It was a little scary when you went away."

"I'm sorry," he repeated. He smiled again and wagged his head playfully. Suddenly his eyes went rigid.

"We have something to discuss." The tone was flat.

Lilly froze. He took her hand and led her into the tent, where they sat facing each other on two chairs borrowed from Ramón's house, which had sustained surprisingly little damage.

Jean took both of her hands in his good one and caressed her fingers gently. He drew his mouth into a forced smile.

"We have lost everything, Lilly. The guesthouse, our house, the fruit trees, the furniture, the radios and appliances." He dropped his head. "Everything."

"What do you want to do? We can stay here and rebuild, we can leave and find another place to live. We could return to the States, although that might not be such a good idea. If we went somewhere completely new in the States, perhaps we'd be okay. We can't go to France. It's just too hot now. But I want you to know that I want to do what you want to do. I know that the storm was a natural disaster, that it wasn't my fault, or anything that I could control, but I feel . . ."

He broke off and squeezed her hands. Lilly lifted his hand to her face and kissed it.

"How could you possibly take responsibility for any of this? You have given us such a wonderful life. I couldn't have imagined it before I came here. Look at the kids. Look at Evie. They are so happy here. They're confident and they've got good friends. Henry especially—he was miserable in Tucson. The only thing that kept him going was that he knew you would call us to you when it was time. You don't know how that kid waited. Waited and waited, every day, for you."

She paused for the importance of the words to sink in.

"But I think you are missing one vital step," she said. "We have to ask the kids. I know they'll do anything we decide together, but we have to ask them."

"Okay, tonight, after dinner. But there is something else."

His tone said she wouldn't like what was coming.

"What?" Her eyes searched his face. He looked down.

"The hurricane destroyed almost the entire infrastructure of the island. Ramón tells me they will rebuild, but it could take months to achieve, possibly years. I have some money in the safe, which survived, thank God. There is enough to live on for a while, but not enough in there to rebuild or even begin. All services to the island will be restored eventually, but our electricity might not be functioning for some time. What we need to rebuild is more cash than I can access right now."

Lilly sat quietly, hearing the conversation, knowing it was going in a dangerous direction. Jean had lived an entire life of crime before they met two years earlier, and she never forgot that. He never talked about it; she never asked. It was the business he knew best and the straightest line to money. What came next was a predictable surprise.

"There's still over four hundred thousand in Tucson. It will be a quick trip; just a couple of days in and out. I will fly into L.A., rent a car, drive to Tucson, and empty the safe-deposit boxes in one day."

Lilly was shaking her head through his whole delivery. It was impossible that he was considering this. He was ignoring her.

"It might be risky to fly into Tucson, and I can't carry the cash on a plane, so I'll leave it with my friend Dominic to send in small packets once the mail is running again. I'll be gone just a couple of days."

His tone told her he had already decided. There was little point in arguing. She trusted Jean. She knew his skill. But collecting the money meant returning to a place he had barely escaped. The authorities had had two years to unearth his identity. It had taken her thirty years to find this man, and she couldn't lose him now.

"Jean . . . please, I don't want you to go. Not now. I need you now, especially now. The kids are still really traumatized, and I'm nervous. I just," she paused looking him hard in the eye, "just don't go. We'll make it. We'll be fine."

"Lilly," Jean said gently. "Lilly, I know what you're saying. It can be dangerous, yes. But I have to go back sometime, and it might be better to go now rather than later. The longer I wait, the longer they have to find information on me. We should have done this a year ago. Safe-deposit boxes are nothing, trust me. It will take ten minutes at each bank. I can do all of them in one day without a problem. I'll map them out and visit them one by one. You have to understand, it's not nearly as risky as you're thinking. Lilly, trust me."

"I do trust you. That's not the point. It's just dangerous. What happens if you get caught?"

Jean looked at her and smiled.

"Remember?" he deflected. He took both of her hands and held them together in his, kissing her fingers. "Remember what you said? You said, 'I'll bet you're a real professional.' Remember?"

"Of course I do. I also remember you didn't like it. I just figured that we would wait more like ten or twelve years, and then you could go and get the money." She dropped her head. "This is just bad timing. I'm scared, the kids are scared."

"Scared? You? Lilly, you're the bravest woman I've ever met. That's one of the reasons I fell in love with you. Besides the fact that you're a sexy woman—I found you irresistible."

He was flirting with her now, and his overture always turned her on. The next kiss took them to the bed fashioned from crates and a mattress that Ramón had stored in his out building. It had been over a week since they had last made love, typically a daily activity.

"Mommy?" Sherri called from outside the tent.

"Arrgghh, kids," Jean groused. Lilly pinched his ass playfully and stood to straighten her clothes.

"What, honey?"

"Henry won't let me crack the coconuts. I just want to crack one."

Lilly glanced back at her husband smiling wickedly at her backside.

"Later, after the kids go to bed," she whispered, and went outside to settle the quarrel.

LaChance lay back in the make-shift bed and stared at the ceiling of the tent. She could be right. It could be dangerous. He knew nothing about Richard Prescott, the man whose money he and Dewey Jensen had stolen. Stolen cash was tough to prove, which was why thieves always dealt in cash. But rich men were powerful men, connected men. LaChance knew. The problem was not the amount of money stolen. The problem was that they had stolen it. Powerful men would spend more than they had lost to catch whoever had taken it.

Another complication occurred to him. It had been two years since that life. He was now a hotel proprietor. He was out of practice. He had not picked a lock or a safe in two years. A professional thief had to keep up with technique, with technology. Most likely, he would not have to break in anywhere. He would walk into the bank, sign the papers, offer his key and walk out with the cash. It would be simple. If only he could convince Lilly of that. If only he could convince himself.

Death of the Frenchman

Chapter 8

A week before LaChance was scheduled to leave, he withdrew from the family to settle his mind. He started to prepare. After dark, he practiced opening locked doors wherever he could find them but was careful to lock them again. No one here could know his true identity. He had become a trusted friend to the community, and he wanted to keep it that way. He recalled telephone numbers, identity information, addresses, social security numbers—anything he might be asked to supply for access to the safe-deposit boxes. His French passport was the only link to his past, and he was not ready to part with that quite yet. On paper, Jean LaChance did not exist.

The year before, he had grown a mustache on Lilly's suggestion. She said it made him look more French. He hadn't shaved at all since the hurricane, and the length of stubble gave him a feral appearance. Standing in front of the mirror, he looked at his face and decided he needed a cleaner look, something respectable. He considered shaving everything, or perhaps just his lower jaw.

The razor was leaning next to the mirror and when he reached for it, the back of his hand knocked it off balance and it fell from the shelf. He snatched at the razor and a lightning bolt shot through his shoulder. He cursed in French and at the same moment, caught his reflection in the mirror.

The face was not his own. It wasn't the week's growth of whiskers or the mustache. The word that erupted spontaneously from his mouth was French, but the mouth no longer belonged to Jean LaChance. The man in the mirror was older. He was out of practice, but more importantly, he was injured.

He had been two years on the island. LaChance had changed his name, his profession, and become a father. Physically, he was in good shape. He had started running, and had quit smoking when Evie was born. Most of his daily life involved physical activity around the guest house or working with Ramón.

But he was injured. His shoulder ached badly, a deep, grinding ache that he knew would not go away with time. It might require surgery, which would take time to heal. Right now, he had no time. They needed money. At least that was what he told Lilly.

He stared at himself in the mirror. The other man stared back. The eyes never lie, but he had lied to Lilly. Did she know? Did she suspect him for an instant?

Jean LaChance had been stoic, hard, calculating. Perfectly capable of lying.

Pierre LaPorte was soft, understanding, a daddy. Trustworthy.

Doubts flickered through LaChance's head. Could he do it? Certainly, if nothing happened the money pick-up in Tucson would be easy. But if something happened . . . it would be bad to be caught at this stage. They would extradite him to France. They could get him on the bank job, and likely several other heists. The Paris Police had been drooling for Jean LaChance for years. He would go to jail for the rest of his life. For the first time in his life, LaChance was petrified to go to work.

"Dad?"

LaChance jumped so hard the razor in his hand crashed to the bowl that served as a sink. His head snapped over at Henry. The boy saw a hard fear in the eyes of a man he did not know.

"That's okay. I didn't mean to bother you," Henry said quickly and turned to leave.

"Henry, come here, it's okay."

The boy turned back to look at his father's face, the trusting face he knew and loved. LaChance smiled and tousled Henry's hair, a private ritual for both.

"What's up?" the man asked.

"Nothin.' Just lookin' for you."

Jean gestured with his head. "Let's take a walk."

He led the boy down to the seashore, where they sat on the white sand and looked out to sea. Gulls wheeled in the air above, expecting a hand out. The gentle blue waves whooshed into the beach with a rhythmic cadence. Jean laid a hand on Henry's shoulder and the two shared their favorite wordless conversation.

Finally, Jean spoke.

"Are you having any bad dreams?"

The boy looked down and kicked his bare feet in the sand. The day they came to the island, Henry had taken his shoes off. Jean hadn't seen them on his feet since that time. Lilly had said nothing.

Death of the Frenchman

"Maybe. Not really. Not a storm, just some crazy chasing stuff. I think Mom has nightmares. Sherri and Amos, too."

"Yeah?"

"Are you having bad dreams?" the boy asked.

Jean's eyes darkened. "Not about hurricanes."

"What are you dreaming about?"

Jean took in a deep breath and blew it out slowly. He held his words for several moments. Henry waited. He could feel his father's struggle.

"You know what I did before? Before we came here?"

"Yeah, kinda. I mean, I know that you and Dewey did that . . . that job and got the money."

The conversation was cryptic. Both of them understood perfectly.

"That life is over for me. At least I think it is. I hope it is. When I met your mother, she—all of you—became more important than anything else. I wasn't particularly proud of what I had done," he broke off.

"It doesn't matter to me," Henry said. He looked up at the man. "Really."

Jean smiled.

Henry smiled back, then turned his attention to the ocean.

"Is that why sometimes you look like a different person?" he asked.

Jean turned to look at the boy. Their eyes met.

"I look like a different person?"

"Yeah."

"Like when?"

"Like just now, when you were shaving."

Jean wrapped his arm around his oldest child. He rested his chin on the boy's head, and encountered bumps on the crown. The curls of Henry's wild hair were becoming dreadlocks.

"You need a haircut, buddy."

"That's what Mom says, but I like it this way."

Jean chuckled.

"I'm sorry I look like somebody else sometimes. I wasn't aware."

"You don't look like somebody else, Dad. You look like you did when I met you, that's all. Not all the time, just when you're thinking about something serious. Like now, after the hurricane."

"Well, I did have another life, before. I was somebody else." Jean paused. "Life is serious now, Henry. The hurricane changed a lot of things." Jean paused.

"Buddy, I have to go back to Tucson. We need money, and I have to go get it. We can't rebuild unless I do."

He felt the boy stiffen.

"I want to go with you."

"No."

"Why not?" the boy asked hotly. "I can do a lot of stuff."

Jean hugged him close.

"I know you can. That's why you can't go. You have to take care of the family. What would they do if both of us left?"

"Oh."

"There's a lot of work to do and Mom is going to need help, especially with the baby."

"Yeah." He paused. "I like Evie. She's cool, huh?"

Jean laughed. "Yeah, she's cool."

"She looks like you."

"Really?" Jean had always thought with relief that the little girl looked like Lilly.

"Yeah, mostly your eyes. Not your nose," Henry teased.

"Thank goodness, huh?" Jean presented his profile, exaggerating his long, sloping beak.

"Yeah, she's got Mom's nose." Henry paused and swept his hand through the sand at his side. "But she's got your personality. She's strong, like you."

Jean took in a deep breath and exhaled in a long sigh.

"You got to help me now, buddy," Jean said. "We have to take care of everybody."

"Okay," Henry said. He shifted his weight on the sand to sit closer to Jean. "I like it when you call me buddy."

"Good. I like it when you call me Dad."

Neither made an attempt to move. Soon, the man would be gone. They wanted this to last as long as possible.

Chapter 9

Guy Santino rolled over and opened his eyes. It felt good to be back in L.A. He preferred a bit of grit in his life. Tucson was far too clean and straight. It would be nice to get back to his practice; think about something besides the Frenchman for a change. The silence from Tucson was agonizing. Santino had stayed for a week, driving around aimlessly, investigating neighbors near Lilly's old house for more information.

One nosy woman had remembered seeing a man with a blue car of some kind, and the timing was perfect. He was tall and thin. He hadn't been there very long, maybe a couple of days, but he had stayed in the house with the family. Maybe he was an uncle, the lady said, but she doubted it. With the rampant immorality these days, who could tell anymore?

Santino had returned to the Tucson Police Department to start the process of gaining access to bank surveillance film. Until he knew which banks, it was fruitless to start looking. Bank policy dictated the term of retention, and many of the smaller banks erased surveillance tapes within several weeks, or even days.

Santino rolled out of bed and padded in bare feet and boxers to the bathroom. He had quit drinking some months earlier when he returned to the Prescott case. The high was no longer necessary now that he had both Lilly Parsons and Jean LaChance to fill his day. Hope had returned and fed something indefinable in his soul. The fatigue he had experienced as a detective with the department had been replaced with energy possessing an endless appetite. It had started the moment he looked into the eyes of Jean LaChance. He studied the photo multiple times a day. If he encountered LaChance, he would recognize the man immediately despite the twenty years elapsed since the time of the mug shot. He examined the face for any unusual characteristics; a mole, a scar. He explored the intense eyes for answers.

The photo also gave Santino a tangible item; not merely the face of the man he had been seeking for two years, but a physical piece of paper he could touch. The photo breathed life into the unsolved case.

Two years before when Santino had finally caught up with Lilly and the kids at her house, an innocent note taped to the refrigerator had blown her departure plans. A flight number and time. Santino had driven Lilly to the airport; walked her to the very gate matching the number on the slip. Santino knew LaChance was close. He knew the ghost was there, in plain sight.

Lilly had strolled down the concourse, sat at a small table near a restaurant and calmly ordered a cup of coffee. He watched her straighten her hair in her compact mirror, then produce a spiral notebook she pretended to read. As soon as the flight was announced, passengers started to move toward the gate and he had lost sight of her several times. Santino had surveyed the passengers near the gate, even pulling a few single men to the side, which caused confusion and riled tempers, but never came across anyone who might be joining Lilly. The number of passengers had dwindled, and with them, any hope of apprehending the ghost. After the flight had departed, he was left with little else but to take Lilly home. Her face was like glass. But somewhere there was a flicker of emotion impossible to interpret. Grief? Resignation? He knew he would never get her to admit anything.

Santino was torn apart with envy for the man who was his prey. Wasn't that true love? Sacrifice, trust, and not the trust signified by spitting or mixing of blood. This was no show. The two of them had displayed blind trust, with no guarantee of resolution. The woman had sacrificed her freedom for that man, and by her own choice. LaChance had simply walked away. Six months later, Lilly and the kids disappeared. Santino was certain they had joined him. Lilly was pregnant. The child had to be LaChance's.

French authorities had not seen any sign of LaChance since the bank job three and a half years before. They assumed he was gone for good. So had Santino.

But LaChance had to come back sometime. There was still a pile of money somewhere. A volume of cash large enough to be conspicuous, too much to deposit in a short amount of time, too risky to hide in a city full of strangers.

Santino didn't give a shit about Richard Prescott and his spare cash. He was no longer after the money. Back then, Board of Commissioners member Nelson Ackerly had provided the motivation to find Prescott's money; harassment and condescension followed by a tempting bribe of early retirement. Times had changed. Right now, no external motivation existed for Santino. His incentive was internal and burned with a blue flame.

Death of the Frenchman

He wanted the guy.

Much of LaChance's lengthy dossier obtained from the Paris Police was speculation. He had only been arrested once, and in his twenties. His most impressive work had taken place in the last ten years, and all over the world. He always worked alone, and had been spending increasing time outside of France. He engaged in specialized crime; jewelry, priceless art, antiques, historically significant items. Everyone in that world knew who he was, but no one knew him.

A target on that level was a first for Santino. He was way out of his element, and he knew it. So why not call the Feds? Certainly Interpol and the FBI would partner to nab a guy like Jean LaChance. He could pass along all the evidence and get LaChance out of his head.

Santino made coffee in the kitchen and sat down at the table with the photo in one hand. He sipped the steaming cup and searched the young LaChance's eyes. Could he pass this up? Probably not.

"Where are you?" he asked the photo. "When are you coming back?"

Little did he know, Jean LaChance was preparing for his return to the U.S. at that very moment.

Chapter 10

Jean threw his bag in the back of the Jeep and turned to face his family. They had not been apart for more than a few hours in the last two years. He wanted a quick-as-possible departure to minimize Lilly's tears and his own guilt. He knew it would be a bad scene, one that he didn't need right now.

Lilly stood in front of their tent-become-make-shift home with the baby propped on her hip. Amos and Sherri stood on either side of their mother looking up at the man who had become their father by choice. Jean knelt like a parishioner begging for redemption.

The pout on Sherri's face threatened to erupt into tears at any moment. Amos was quiet, as usual, but sullen. Jean embraced them, one in each arm. The tears came.

"I'll be back soon, I promise," he said.

He kissed side to side repeatedly and stood to face Lilly. Her mouth was drawn in a tight line. Her biceps bulged from under her T-shirt. Evie was a heavy kid, and the constant lifting had kept her strong. Suddenly, she was the tomboy mother of the kids out in the California desert, surviving day to day on gophers, her steely mentality holding up the earth like Atlas every day for her children.

Though she was silent, two steady streams ran from her eyes to her chin and dripped periodically to the front of her shirt. Her expression was flat resignation. She knew she could do nothing to stop him, because she had tried, many times. She had begged, threatened and even tried seduction and withholding sex. Nothing would change his mind.

As the days ticked closer to his departure, she had watched him revert from her loving husband and the devoted father of her children to the professional criminal he had been a lifetime ago. He disappeared for hours, especially after dark. She had no idea where he went, and when she asked him, he ignored her. At times he sat stock-still in a chair, staring ahead into space, fixed on a target invisible to everyone else. She didn't bother to ask what he was doing. She didn't want to know. When their eyes met, she felt she didn't know him. He was distant, withdrawn. Not the man she had married.

When he did return to present time, he reserved it for the kids, who were unable to understand why he was leaving. He played games with them on the sandy path in front of the tent. Giddy laughter floated through the canvas walls and crushed Lilly's heart. Logically, she knew it made sense. Emotionally, it tore her apart. The memory of the man she had met at the house in the desert came back in a rush. That man had been devoid of emotion, which was an intriguing aspect of his character. It had been sexy and challenging. Now, it was simply heart-breaking.

Over two years, Jean had metamorphosed into a warm, understanding partner, husband and father. He dealt as easily with Sherri and Evie as he did with the boys. He laughed. He played. He made love with sensual abandon. He did everything completely, including the retreat to his former life.

He stood before her now with a distant expression of guilt, determination and nerves. She could see his suffering, and his reluctance to show it. He lifted Evie from Lilly's arms, kissed her chubby cheek, and handed the baby to Amos.

"Come on," he ordered. He held out his hand.

Lilly folded her arms across her chest and brushed past his outstretched hand. They walked down the street, arms-length apart to a path leading to the beach. Lilly was crying. Tears hung from her chin and the end of her nose, but she didn't make a sound.

He waited to speak until they were on the sand, where he gestured for her to sit down. He faced her cross-legged and drew her knees as close as possible to his. He leaned forward and took her face into his hands. She collapsed into sobs.

Jean watched her without a trace of emotion, like he was reading a newspaper. She cried for a while, then sniffled and blew her nose. They were finally alone, out of earshot of the village and the children.

"What do you want me to say?" she asked fiercely.

"Nothing. Nothing at all. Anything you want."

The flood of emotion erupted from Lilly.

"I'm so angry at you, Jean. You tell me you're leaving and then you retreat into your hidden world where I can't join you, and you only come out for the kids. Every night you turn your back to me in bed. I don't know what's going on, and you don't tell me. Now in just minutes, you're leaving and God knows how long you'll be gone, or if you'll ever come back. It could be two days. It could be two months. I know you're going back to get the money you and Dewey stole, but you're not telling me anything about it, where you'll be, who you're meeting, what you'll do. We have no way of knowing if anyone is there laying a trap for you, and if they catch you, I'll never know. You'll simply disappear. And I'll be here with the kids alone and we'll never hear from you again."

She paused, her chest heaving. Their eyes were locked together, neither able to look away to relieve the tension. She was grasping for control of her emotions and losing the battle with every sentence. She took a deep breath.

"I just . . . just don't understand how you can do that to us. After all this, after what we've been through and what it took for us to be together. So what if we don't have enough money to rebuild? So what? So, we'll do something else, but we'll be together. I . . . I think what you're doing is so selfish and . . . unnecessary. The hurricane was bad enough, but now you punish me with this, and I'm . . . I'm beginning to hate you. The kids don't know what's going on. You always say it has to be a mutual decision, but you decided this, and nobody else gets to weigh in. I asked you to ask the kids. Did you? No. Henry said you told him you were going. What about that, Jean? What about that?"

Her voice was escalating, both in volume and intensity. He reached a hand up to touch her face. She jerked away.

"I don't want you to go, the kids don't want you to go, but you're going, nonetheless. I don't understand. It's like you've lost your mind, and we, the kids and me have to pay the price for your insanity."

Jean sat silently and listened to the cruel words that stabbed his heart repeatedly. She was right. It wasn't fair. He waited until she ran out of punishment and wound down to a stop.

"You're right, Lilly. I know you're right. What's been happening with us is . . . inevitable, and it's my fault. I have to go back to my past life to be able to do this successfully. I'm out of practice. I haven't handled a gun or accessed a lock for two years. This requires preparation; mentally, physically. I can't walk into it cold, or it's certain that I'll be caught. But I'm ready, Lilly."

He ducked his head down and lifted her face with his hand. "I'm ready."

"And now you're going."

"Yes, I'm going. I'm sorry this has been hard on you. In order for me to get back to LaChance, I can't be affected by any emotion that might make me weak or vulnerable. Don't you see? You are my love, Lilly. You are my world. You and the kids. I also believe in your strength and your trust—in me. I know your strength and that you can bear all of this. If I didn't think you could, I wouldn't go."

"Then don't go. Stay for us. At least then we'll be together."

Jean dropped his head in guilt.

"I have to go, Lilly. I have to do this. I don't know why, but I feel that I have to do this and close that chapter."

He raised his head and looked into her eyes.

"It will be okay. Just a couple of days. I'll walk into the banks and get the money. They won't know a thing, really. Trust me, Lilly. Trust me. If there is a problem, I'll know, and I'll walk away."

"Why do you keep asking me to do more than I've done already? Why do you insist on insulting me? Obviously I trust you Jean. I came here, didn't I? I made plane reservations based on a picture post card with one word written on the front, and I dragged three little kids thousands of miles not sure where we were going or what was at the end. I was seven months pregnant. I left my entire life behind, not that it was much of a life, but I left it. Left it and came to this island because you called me. I had known you one fucking week and I did it anyway. Against my better judgment. I did for me, of course, but I did it for the kids, and I fucking did it for you."

She was screaming by this time, and tears were streaming down her cheeks.

"So just go and get it over with!"

She wrenched her hands away from his grip. He grabbed for them, but she had thrown them into the air out of his reach.

"Go back to your life of crime that you think you've sacrificed for us. Go be . . . be that person again; that life that you so badly need to return to. But don't act like you're the only one who has sacrificed."

Sobbing had taken her speech, and she was barely able to get the words out.

"You know . . . you know what I want to know? I want to know what ha . . . happens to us if you don't come back? Am I su . . . supposed to just live here? Am I supposed to go back to the States? My life here is noth . . . nothing without you here. So just go and fucking get it over with!"

She stood and turned her back on him, walking defiantly down the beach without one sign of turning around. He watched her—her words sticking like a knife in his chest. He ached to run after her, hold her tightly and promise that nothing bad would happen. A terrible weight out of his control kept him rooted to the sand.

Death of the Frenchman

The sound of an engine caught Jean's attention and he turned to see his friend Ramón, his ride to the airport. Time had run out. Emotion rose into his throat and he choked back a sob. She was right. He was being selfish. He was risking their life together. But a fanatical force had driven him to this end, and he knew it was no longer about the money at all. He looked back to Lilly. She was far down the beach, still putting distance between them.

Jean got up and brushed the sand off his pants. He turned and walked up the beach, shook hands with Ramón and looked toward the tent. Amos and Sherri were standing looking at him. Sherri was crying. Henry was nowhere to be seen. He had been gone before they had gotten up that morning. Jean was glad. Leaving Lilly was hard enough, but she had given him an exit with the harsh, truthful words. He knew he deserved it. Henry might have given him worse, and Jean was glad to be spared that scene. He climbed in the passenger's side of the Jeep. Ramón slipped it into gear and started for the airport. When Jean looked back to Lilly, she was a speck in the distance, still walking the other direction.

Chapter 11

As soon as they arrived at the airport, LaChance crossed the road and entered the Hot Spot Bar where he had waited every day for three weeks for Lilly and the kids to arrive two years earlier. He saw Margaret, the bartender, around the village on occasion, and they always exchanged little pleasantries and warm smiles, their shared visits from the past.

"'Ello, Mr. Pierre. 'Ow are you doing this fine day?" Margaret asked.

"Thank you, Margaret, I am well," Jean said. "May I have a pack of Camels?"

Jean hadn't smoked for almost two years. The transition back to LaChance was nearly complete. Margaret rang up the sale, and he opened the pack immediately, stuck a cigarette in his mouth and accepted the lighter held up for him.

"Thank you. I'm leaving for a little while. You take care," Jean said.

"I have heard about this," Margaret said, with a worried look. "May God go with you."

Jean smiled and blew out a long line of blue smoke. It felt good to smoke again. Of course, Lilly would be angry. He hoped she had stopped crying.

He returned to the Jeep to fetch his bag.

"Thank you for bringing me," Jean said flatly. His face was strained.

"De nada."

"Ramón, please look in on Lilly and the kids every couple of days, will you? She's not very happy with me right now, and, well . . ."

"Of course, I will," the man interrupted. His soft brown eyes conveyed concern. They stood in silence for a while. Ramón finally spoke.

"Mr. Pierre, I don't know what you're going to do in the States, but I assume it must be dangerous. I suspected you were running from something when you came here—many expats are. But you're different. There's something more about you.

And you have a family. Your children depend on you. Please be careful. Please come back to us. Your family is too important. But then you know that."

Jean took in the advice without reply. He was a bit angry that the man would cross the line into his personal world, but Ramón was a trusted friend. Jean could forgive him that.

"You know, you could change your mind right now," Ramón added, gesturing toward the Jeep. "There would be no shame in that."

Jean took a long drag from his cigarette. It was tempting. But as soon as he allowed in that smidgen of doubt, his stomach clamped with disgrace. There would be no going back.

"Thank you," Jean said. "I'll be back soon."

"Good," Ramón said. "Good. Take good care, my friend. Vaya con Dios."

"Merci. Vaya con Dios."

Jean lifted his bag out of the Jeep. Ramón shifted into drive and pulled away. Jean watched the Jeep disappear before turning to walk to the building. Flights had just begun to return to the island following the hurricane. The cement block building was strong and had survived with very little damage, although all the palm trees in the vicinity had been stripped of their fronds. The wreckage of several small planes in a twisted pile still remained near the airstrip as a bleak testimony.

The sing-song voices of the airport attendants greeted him from behind the desk. His flight took off in a half hour. He had plenty of time. He bought a cup of coffee and sat down to wait. Lilly's poisonous words raged through his mind. Why had those words been her last? He had wanted to hold her and kiss her and remember her that way, but he had given her the choice and she had castigated him to the end.

What you're doing is so selfish. I'm beginning to hate you.

It was the first time he had ever heard those words directed at him; stinging words that cut him deeply. Selfishness required a relationship, and Lilly was technically his first. He closed his eyes and squeezed back the tears. He had to get them out of the way to clear the path for the professional to come back into power. He wasn't quite there yet, but he would be. That afternoon at the mirror, he had felt the fear of doubt. The doubt of the ability to make the transition, which could then endanger his mission and his life. He sucked in a deep breath. He needed another cigarette.

The door overlooking the airstrip opened to the west. Beyond the airstrip was a line of scrubby brush and trees ravaged by the storm. LaChance walked out the door and lit up, letting his gaze drift from one end of the airstrip to the other.

Death of the Frenchman

Suddenly a movement in the vegetation on the other side caught his eye. He looked carefully, but whatever had caused the flicker was gone. He finished his cigarette and walked back inside.

The plane was twenty minutes late, and as soon as the arriving passengers filed through the building, they began boarding. Jean turned and looked back in the direction of the village, feeling the tug of his present life, but resigned to the choice he had made. The few passengers boarded and Jean finally forced himself to walk up the angled steps and find a seat. The plane taxied out to the end of the airstrip, wound up its engines and began the race to the far end. Just as the wheels left the ground, Jean looked out his window and caught that same movement down below that he had seen from the building. It was Henry, standing by the edge of the runway, dirty smears down his cheeks, waving his hand frantically to the plane taking his father away.

Chapter 12

Lilly had cried so long her tear ducts were dry and scratchy. She walked the beach until she was out of sight of the village. Finally, she turned and looked back the way she had come. The long white beach was empty.

Jean was gone.

Over the past two years the island had become Lilly's sanctuary; a secure haven containing all the ingredients of happiness. Suddenly, all that had changed. It was a prison now, and her sentence would last until Jean returned from his illicit errand.

She dropped down in the sand and stared out to sea. Guilt swam in her gut for leaving Amos in charge of the girls, but he was a responsible kid and knew what to do. He was ten years old now, the age that Henry had been when Jean first drove up to the house in the desert. He changed Evie's diapers and fed her when she was hungry.

The two boys couldn't be more different. Henry was sharp and reactive; Amos was quiet and thoughtful. Henry was physical, athletic; Amos was a book-worm. He had read more books than the whole family put together. They had both done an excellent job with child care, but Amos had a care-taking instinct that was sweet and served the family well in their guest house. He filled the role of youth manager, covering the phone and talking with the guests, with baby Evie in tow.

Henry had been gone when Lilly awoke that morning. It was not unusual. He hustled jobs around the village for his own money, and never asked for anything. He had passed the caretaker's torch to Amos as soon as Evie was born, which was more than fair. Henry had been in charge of his siblings for almost four years. His brown locks had grown out of control and gave him a wild appearance. Lilly had attempted to cut it, but he refused to let her touch his head.

Naturally, now that they were together, Jean had taken over as man of the house, and Henry's emancipation was immediate. Lilly missed their private talks, but Henry showed no need for that lost element of their relationship. He rarely spoke with her.

The boy worked closely with Jean in the property maintenance. Anything mechanical came easily to him. Jean had assigned him certain regular tasks, and Henry completed them without additional instruction or reminders. Lilly knew they didn't talk much, either. They had had a silent code from the beginning. They understood each other, like two psychics holding separate, yet connected, séances. Lilly was furious at Jean's departure, but she knew Henry could, and would hold his anger much longer.

She rolled onto her back and stretched in the sand, coaxing her strained muscles to relax. When her hands folded on her stomach, she glimpsed her wedding ring, set with four white diamonds, one each for the kids.

Jean and Lilly had been married in June two years earlier on a secluded beach at the far west side of the island. Lilly purchased a floral print island dress for the ceremony. Jean wore a white linen shirt and khaki trousers. Besides the priest from a neighboring island, the kids were the only guests in the private ceremony. Sherri carried flowers, and Amos was the ring-bearer. Henry served as best man, the sole attendant in his parents' wedding. A lazy sun sat low on the horizon, preparing for sunset, and they spoke their vows in hushed tones, witnessed only by the kids and three wheezing gulls. Lilly was quite pregnant by that time, and Jean held her hands in one of his, placing his free hand on her belly during his vows, which promised to care for her and the kids until death took him from the earth.

A deep sob jumped to her throat. The searing anger had dissolved into a clutching void of loneliness and fear. Her last words to him ravaged her soul.

I'm beginning to hate you.

The words screamed in her head. She couldn't believe she had said them. Thank God the kids hadn't heard. Jean had sat looking at her face, absorbing the vile words, making no attempt to stop her tirade. He knew he had to hear them. He had allowed her the freedom of emotional release, in fact, had welcomed it. It was necessary for her to drive him away. It gave him permission to leave.

Lilly watched the cumuli drift on the trade winds announcing the change of season. It occurred to her that she didn't even know under what name Jean was traveling, whether he was American or French, his flight plan, or where he would be staying. Rage had taken over, and forced her to release her fury on the man she loved. And now he was gone and it was impossible to retrieve any of it.

Death of the Frenchman

How long would he be gone? The phones would be down for weeks, so there would be no news until the system was restored. He had said "a couple of days." Impossible. It took two days to reach the States. Would it be a week? Two? When should she start to worry? She suddenly realized the worry had begun as soon as he told her he was going.

A glance at the sun, now past its zenith, told her it was time to go home. Home. It was a damn tent. They would be camping until they could rebuild. She was finally calm; her emotions, depleted.

Jean had taken care of business before he left. He had set her up with a cook stove and improvised appliances, which made it possible to function. He had shown her where the money was, had coached her on the expenses and vital chores. He had rigged an outside shower and cleaned out the cistern that had saved their lives to supply them with fresh water. He had set up the generator and made sure Henry could start and run it. He had coordinated with his friend Ramón to look after them. He had done all of that in the midst of the retreat into his former life.

During his absence, there was little more to do than wait. Lilly had seen his wounded face as she raged her insecurities at him. He held it together even with his shoulder injury and was now placing himself in the path of the maelstrom for all of them. He wasn't doing it for only himself; he was also doing it for them.

Lilly lifted her head as the wind shifted and brought the pitch of a prop plane. The sound rose and grew as it approached the beach, and suddenly, the plane banked high over the beach in the direction of Venezuela, carrying her husband away. Lilly shaded her eyes, waving her fingers slowly, in the hope that he might be looking down. Then she dropped her head into the sand, and sobbed.

Chapter 13

Lilly was stumbling through a painful, sad, unhurried daydream. She returned to the tent exhausted, but resolute to keep as busy as she could for as long as she could. She stepped inside the tent. Everything she saw also revealed Jean's face, and she erupted into tears. She shook and sobbed for her breath and pounded her knees red.

Amos and Sherri were playing outside with Evie. Thank God. The baby was in safe hands.

A glance around the tent only tired her. The kids should be fed, but she wasn't a bit hungry. She would think about it later. The bed beckoned her, and she gave in without a second thought. Her outburst and hours of tears had left her hollow, and she was out in seconds. Disturbing scenes of pursuit and near-misses flooded her dreams, and she jerked awake veiled in sweat.

Late afternoon sun illuminated the broad side of the tent, creating the illusion of electric light. Lilly lay still for several minutes, wincing into her headache, feeling hung-over. He was gone. Probably in Venezuela already.

Why did this have to happen now? Evie was only a baby, and required watchful, full-time eyes. The temporary living situation was stressful, but had been tolerable with her husband alongside. Jean's absence was already overwhelming. An empty ache in her chest made it hard to breathe.

Her pounding head forced her to her feet. She poured a glass of water from the thermal jug on the table. The liquid resuscitated her scratchy throat and soothed her nerves. Sounds from the outside drew her attention. From her seat at the table she could just see through the crack of the tent flap.

Amos and Sherri were sitting across the road with their legs encircling the baby, playing patty-cake over her head. Evie squealed with delight at the end of every verse, and clapped her hands for them to do it again. Lilly smiled and shook her head. She wanted to feel sorry for herself. She did feel that she was sorry, pretty damn sorry. Everything could be a lot worse. The kids were dealing with this much better than she. It was time to grow up.

She stood up and pushed the tent flap aside.

"Hey you guys!" she yelled.

"Hi Mommy!" Sherri returned. Evie screeched when she saw her mother.

"Let's go to the beach."

They spent the rest of the late afternoon splashing in the blue surf of the Caribbean Sea. Childish spontaneity eased Lilly's anxiety, and life rewound to the time that she and the kids had been alone together. By the time the sun disappeared behind the crest of the island, they were tired and hungry and ready for a quiet evening.

Lilly hummed to herself as pasta grew soft and fat in the pot on the propane cook stove. The hiss of the stove accompanied Amos' narration of the current book. He lay on the bed with the book propped on his stomach, embellishing the story with imaginary facts, characters and voices just as Henry had done so many times for him. The improvised result was usually better than the original story. The kids had no idea how creative they were, and it made Lilly beam. She checked the clock on the tent upright and jumped when she saw it was after seven. It had been dark for over an hour, and Henry was still gone.

Lilly was worried, but understanding about the boy. Jean had been his salvation; a real father—for the first time in Henry's life. They had bonded immediately. They were so similar they could intuit each other's actions. Henry more than Lilly understood Jean's departure.

The four sat down to eat around the small table, trying not to notice the empty chairs. Lilly was attempting to avoid the clock face, but it seemed to possess a magnetic power that controlled her eyes. Dinner finished and bedtime followed without a complaint. She was free to worry full time. In the tent, she sat staring at the clock, painting dramatic scenarios for both Jean and Henry in her mind, when she suddenly threw down the wash cloth and escaped into the night.

An orange gibbous moon was peeking over the flat line of the sea. Lilly carried her wine glass across the road and down to the beach. Only here was she spared the scene of Stephanie's carnage; the beach appeared as it had before the storm. She and Jean had sat many nights on the same stretch of sand, discussing the kids, the future, the guest house, and on several occasions, making love on a fleece blanket. He must be in Caracas by now. She wondered what he was doing. She prayed he wasn't angry. She deserved it if he was.

"Hey," said a voice from behind. Lilly jumped.

"Sorry," Henry said, and flopped down beside his mother on the sand. His T-shirt and shorts were filthy, like he had been crawling through brush.

"Hi honey!" she said. She wrapped her arm around his neck and kissed him repeatedly on the head. "I was wondering when you'd come home. Man, you need a haircut, buddy."

"Nope, I like it this way."

"I was worried about you," she said, knowing that he would bristle if she asked him where he had been.

"I know. Sorry."

"That's okay. It's been a hard day."

"Yeah."

A realization struck her like a slap now that he was here. It had been months since she and Henry had really talked. Jean had taken over as his primary parent, and Lilly had been relieved of Henry-duty while she cared for the baby. She was out of practice. Just like Jean. The last two years with the fearless LaChance had left her a less effective parent. Perhaps it was time to regain that skill.

"Did you get something to eat?"

"Not really."

"Are you hungry?"

"Kinda. I brought some fish home."

What a good boy. He never came home empty-handed.

"Let's go back. I kept some supper for you."

"Thanks, but not yet. We should just sit here for a while."

Lilly threw her arm around his shoulders, and he snuggled against her like old times.

"How did you know where to find me?"

"I know where you go. You and Dad come down here all the time after dark."

"Oh." Lilly hoped he had not seen them having sex, and then decided that it probably didn't matter. Henry had always been mature for his age. She was sure he knew about things like sex.

"It's so sweet when you call him Dad. He really likes that, you know."

"Yeah, I know. He told me."

"That's good."

She fell silent for a while, unable to think of anything suitable to say.

"Mom?"

"Yeah honey."

"You shouldn't worry so much about him. He knows what he's doing. He wouldn't do anything stupid. Sometimes I think you worry about him too much. You worry about us kids too much, too."

Lilly shifted her weight in the sand. Henry's wisdom always came in one or two sentences, always a surprise.

"I just love him so much. I love all of you. Mothers can't control how much they worry most of the time. It's our job."

"I guess."

"It's too bad you didn't see him before he left this morning."

"I saw him."

"Really?" Lilly asked. "Where?"

"At the airport, when the plane was taking off."

Lilly was shocked. The airport was over ten miles away. She shook her head in the darkness. He was so much like Jean. A distance like that would mean nothing to Henry if he put his mind to it. He changed the subject.

"Dad showed me lots of things before he left. I can start the generator if you want, and help you with the propane tank for the stove if it runs out, but it's pretty full right now, so it should last a long time."

He looked up at her face.

"You have to trust him, Mom. He would never leave us." He dropped his head, and Lilly almost lost his next comment.

"Not like my real dad did."

He was right, of course. She did have to trust Jean. Her face burned with shame, and she forced back the tears trying to push over her lower lids.

"He told me it would only be a little while. We have to rebuild, Mom. He's smart and he can do anything. You should stop worrying. He needs for us to be strong while he's gone."

"Is that what he said?"

"Not really. Kinda. I just know that's what he was thinking."

"You sure do know what he's thinking. Way more than I do. I was a little hard on him before he left. I was feeling angry and I didn't want him to leave."

"That's okay, Mom. He can take it. I was mad at him, too."

"You really love him, don't you, honey?"

"Yep. He loves us too." He paused and took a deep breath. "He really loves Evie."

"Oh, honey, please don't be jealous of Evie. I know he loves all of you kids equally."

"That's okay. Evie's his baby. That's pretty natural, if you ask me."
"He depends on you, though."
"He depends on you too, Mom."
She tousled his hair and threw her face back in the moonshine.
"You're right. You're right about a lot of things."
Henry sat quietly and dug his toes into the cool sand.
"Don't be scared, Mom. He'll never leave us. He's coming back as soon as he can."
The boy's words rang in her head. She embraced him with both arms and kissed the top of his scruffy dreadlocks.
"Let's go get you something to eat."

Chapter 14

The LAN Airbus left the ground just as a sliver of sun climbed from the horizon and was swallowed by an infinite bank of dark clouds. Thin rain lines streaked the small oval glass panes. The lights of Caracas, Venezuela vanished behind the gray screen, like a million candles being snuffed. Jean laid his temple against the window, seeking relief for his pounding hangover. Last night had been a train wreck on the streets of the city. Car horns, vendors and relentless Spanish babbling had overloaded his senses and driven him to a bar, where he soaked his wounds in half a bottle of Scotch. On the island, a daily glass of red wine with Lilly had been sufficient sensory alteration. He was high on her and the kids, on the life they had created in paradise.

Most nights after the kids were in bed, he and Lilly snuggled on the veranda swing, sipping wine and talking about nothing. It was an easy task to conjure a vision of her—laughing eyes and wet lips. His fingers wound through her curls. She teased him about his serious nature until he was forced to laugh. As the wine drained from their glasses, the talk became sensual, and inevitably, they ended up in a frantic tangle. Jean would pick her up off the swing and throw her onto the day bed under the veranda window, where he would stand over her and strip his shirt off button by button before lowering his weight onto his elbows and sending her into orbit.

The erotic fantasy compounded his headache. What a fool he had been. He knew Lilly well enough to know he was obligated to consult her. She was right. He had failed. The internal struggle of his two personas had rendered him incapable of caring what she thought. He fought to retain the vision of her beautiful smile, but it morphed cruelly into the sight of her back to him, walking away, willing him to leave.

I'm beginning to hate you. . . . so selfish . . . so selfish . . . I'm beginning to hate you.

The torture continued all day and night and dogged him into the next morning. All the phone lines were still down, so he couldn't even call her upon his arrival in the States. Once again, he was alone, but this time, he was desperately lonely.

The night before, a hooker marked him at the bar when she realized how drunk he was, and pressed her breasts against him in a most effective sales pitch. There was nothing more vulnerable than a lonely, drunk man. They were always the easiest targets. LaChance was so wounded he started to leave with the woman, then fled from her outside the door when the night air hit his sweaty forehead. He ran back to the hotel where he threw himself on the bed and slammed his fists into the pillow damp with his own tears. It was only the third time he cried since his mother had died. He had been nine years old. The other was when Evie was born.

He had to make this right. He would get the money as quickly as possible, box it and mail it to his friend Dominic in L.A., to be sent later to the island when mail service had resumed. Then, he would return straightaway to the island, take Lilly into his arms and promise to never leave. He would mean it. She would understand.

The painful vision of her back on the beach returned and the doubt wormed its way in. What if she didn't understand? What if he returned and she and the kids were gone? The story that he had written for himself might not play out. Panic surged through his chest and sent his heart racing. His whole life had been risk; risk of making a mistake, risk of being arrested, risk of being killed. None of it had fazed him. The risk of losing Lilly was terrifying, and with each mile that separated them, the more he realized it could happen. His inherent confidence was eroding with the thought of losing her.

Fitful sleep finally found LaChance, and he twitched and groaned against the window until the wheels touched down on the runway in Lima, Peru. He had a two-hour layover to find some food for his hollow stomach and make the connection to Los Angeles. Pierre LaPorte would clear customs at LAX in time for dinner.

Chapter 15

The phone rang just after eight in the morning and Santino jumped to answer it. Within minutes he was throwing clothes into a satchel for another trip to Tucson.

Jean LaChance's photo had been circulated among bank personnel throughout the city. Morning meetings were convened with a huge projection of the Frenchman's face on the screen of conference rooms, until all staff were briefed. For weeks, there had been no word from the Tucson Police Department. Santino was beginning to lose hope. Two years was a long time. Who would remember one customer among thousands after two years? He had given them LaChance's profile. LaChance was French. He might speak with an accent. His face was memorable, but maybe he had disguised himself. Santino simply had to wait and hope that someone would remember him from the photograph taken thirty years earlier.

Then Patty, a bank officer at the First National Bank, returned from her vacation to New York City. She was full of stories about the towering buildings and the exquisite theaters and museums. She was the only bank employee who had not yet seen the photo of LaChance. She received a private showing in a conference room with the bank president, Thomas Hutchins.

Though Hutchins was a nice, conservatively dressed gentleman about seventy, and decent to his employees, Patty was edgy. He was The President. He explained the reason for the private showing, but it still felt like she was being summoned to the principal's office. She jabbered nervously about her vacation, including details of the flight and her arrival at LaGuardia, where the concourses were so long and congested, she thought she would never get to the bus stand.

"I couldn't believe how many people there were!" Patty squealed.

"Yeah?" Hutchins was trying to ignore her, and focused on the envelope that held the thief's photo.

"It was just amazing walking down the street in that city. People of every color, race, class. It really is America's melting pot."

"Yes, I'm sure that's true," Hutchins agreed, pushing the photo into the woman's hands, wishing he could shove it into her mouth.

Patty took the photo. As soon as her eyes fell on LaChance's face, she reacted visibly.

"Oh, wow," she said. "Who is this? He looks familiar, I think."

"You know him?"

"Yes, yes, I've spoken with him, maybe here at the bank, but I don't . . . remember exactly . . ."

"This photo was taken thirty years ago," Hutchins said. "This man would be about fifty now."

"Hmmm. That may change things," she said, studying the photo.

She hummed to herself and touched the picture.

"There is something, something here," she said. "When did he come into the bank?"

"Two years ago this month."

"Two years!" she said. Her eyes traveled up, down and around the photo. "Let's see . . . yes! Yes, I talked to this man. He was so nice, and had an excellent memory. He had all the numbers memorized. I couldn't believe it. That's why I remember him."

"What was his transaction?"

"Let's see, what was it? Yeah, he opened an account because, hmmm, because he . . . he wanted to rent a safe-deposit box! That's right. It was a safe-deposit box. He was traveling, so I thought it was odd. I was respectful, of course, and didn't ask any nosy questions."

"You don't remember his name, do you?"

"Um, what was it? It was a real American name, like John Jones. We could always look at the records. Not that many safe-deposit boxes are rented. I know I would recognize his name if I heard it. He was very nice. By the way, Mr. Hutchins, what did he do? Why do you want his identity?"

"I'm afraid that's restricted, Patty."

"Wow, did he do something wrong? I find that hard to believe, Mr. Hutchins. He was so nice."

"Yes, well, we should get those records for you. Maybe you can identify his name."

"I'll sure try, Mr. Hutchins. I'm so glad I can help."

Hutchins took her into his office, where her nerves caused even more mindless yakking. Hutchins interrupted her prattle when he found the records for the month of October of that year. She fell silent as she perused the paperwork, her New York manicured fingernails tapping an erratic tempo on the table. Hutchins was about to ask her to stop, when she squeaked.

"Here it is! Here it is, Mr. Hutchins. David Smith. Yes, yes, I remember. He had to open an account because he wanted to rent a box."

Her eyes lit up with pride and she handed the record to Mr. Hutchins, then waited for the praise she was sure would follow. Hutchins took the paper without a word, and sat down quickly at his computer to search for activity on the account. There was nothing at all.

"Can I do anything else for you, Mr. Hutchins? Do you want me to write a report on our transaction; anything I can remember about him?"

"No, thank you, Patty. That's all for now. I'll let you know if there's anything else you can do. Please close the door when you go out. Thank you."

With that, Hutchins was done with Patty. She stood still for several seconds before realizing she had been dismissed. She excused herself softly, but Hutchins didn't even notice her leave the room. He was busy finding the phone number for the Tucson Police. LaChance was a particularly significant crook. International.

This disclosure would be very good for his career.

Chapter 16

"Next please."

The monotone voice summoned Pierre LaPorte to the customs counter at LAX. His open bag revealed two changes of men's clothing; casual, typical. Atypically, this particular traveler's bag contained no money.

The officer's halfhearted "enjoy your stay" were magic words to the man's ears. Jean visibly relaxed. He was in. Traveling on a French passport as Pierre LaPorte, he felt moderately safe, but there was always a chance—and that made him nervous.

Only once and long ago, Lilly had shared the story about her day with the detectives in Tucson; the day Santino had finally caught up with her. Jean was busy stashing the money in safe-deposit boxes. The kids were at school. The detectives had threatened her, scoured the house—and found nothing.

Nothing but a note with the U.S. Airways flight number and time.

The innocent, unintended scrap of paper beckoned Detective Santino from across the room to the front of the refrigerator. Lilly had jotted it down just in case she wouldn't remember it. After that day, she could rattle off U.S. Airways flight number 2946, departing four-fifty from Tucson to Houston, even upon waking from a dead sleep. Lilly had punished herself profoundly for the misstep.

With one shot to identify the accomplice, Santino left the kids with Jose and took Lilly alone to the airport. Lilly held her breath and her head high, praying they had nothing on her. Her best strategy was to keep her mouth shut. The absence of a logical strategic approach left Santino to improvise the impromptu trip. Though he utilized all of his interrogation tactics on the long stifling ride through the snarl of Tucson traffic, nothing worked. She played the mother ignoring a petulant child. Brilliantly. Santino was ready to throw a tantrum by the time they pulled up at departures.

The U.S. Airways concourse swarmed with travelers, making anonymity an easy game. Santino expected to ID the accomplice—somehow. By her reaction? An emotional outburst? He wasn't sure, but Lilly was. Santino was forced to send her in alone to minimize suspicion. She strode down the center of the concourse while Santino attempted to relax against a wall, scrutinizing the crowd.

Was it that one? No. Wait. That one? No.

She made it to the café table without a single sign of contact, pulled a compact from her bag and proceeded to preen. There were many single men—the eyes of most trailed Lilly. Of course, she was a beautiful young woman with a sexy, athletic body, and she had worked that concourse runway like a pro. Santino stamped his feet and cursed the poison of male testosterone.

A tinny voice blared the flight number over the PA. Movement was immediate, and the cops began to lose track of who had been sitting or waiting where. Milling ensued. Lilly was too far off to the side to check regularly. There was one guy—he had looked closely at Lilly, so Santino pulled him to the side and handed him over to the back-up officer from Tucson. The guy blew up; impatient, emotional, loud airport scene. Perfect unintended diversion. Santino lost track of Lilly again. The line dwindled and the passengers boarded. Following an identity check, they released the infuriated customer to board last.

Santino glanced around with clenched fists. The vicinity of the gate was deserted. Lilly still sat at the café table, a small smirk on her face meant for the detective. His eyes swept the concourse and found nothing in particular. She picked up her purse and flipped it over her shoulder.

"Time to go home?" she asked, and pushed ahead of him toward the terminal.

How close Santino had come. A couple hundred feet.

Jean remembered; he had watched the detective from his seat before getting up and heading to another concourse.

After the detectives left Tucson, Lilly never heard from them again, so perhaps the case had been closed. Jean's only use of the name Pierre LaPorte in the States was for travel. David Smith had rented the safe-deposit boxes. As long as the authorities did not investigate the banks, he was safe. They would have assumed that he stashed the money somewhere, but where?

L.A. was just as Jean remembered: hectic, loud, flaky. The clothing was outrageous, the hair, fashion extreme. He strode along the concourse, comfortable to take his time and focus on his environment. He had slept the entire flight from Lima to L.A., and was feeling much better. The hangover was gone. He stopped

Death of the Frenchman

at a payphone and dialed Dominic's number from memory. Dominic answered on the third ring.

"Dominic. Jean."

"Jean! How are you, my friend?"

"I am fine, thank you. I'm in L.A."

Dominic gave Jean directions and the men hung up. Phone conversations would remain short during his time in the States.

The rental car company gave him a plain Chevy sedan, creamed coffee brown, with a large trunk. Having just arrived from a small island where he was known to most of the residents, he faced the shock of population density. The perilous ride to Dominic's house took forty minutes in noisy, heavy but amazingly fast traffic which left Jean sweating and chilled, opening and closing the windows at turns to regulate the temperature and shut out the cacophony of the city. This was not island life. By the time he arrived, he was shattered and wishing he had stayed home.

The man who answered the door was a little older than Jean remembered, but he was the same Dominic, same shoulder-length brown-black hair, piercing black eyes and hearty handshake. He embraced Jean warmly, and soon were sitting in the garden drinking beer. Jean opened with business.

"I'll need another passport," he said. He always kept one passport ahead.

"Done," Dominic said. "American?"

"Maybe Canadian, this time," Jean said. "They're allowed to go anywhere."

"Name?"

"Something generic. I appreciate the French flavor, you know, but it's a little close for comfort. Living with Lilly and the kids this whole time has been good for my American accent."

Dominic laughed.

"I'm going to Tucson to make a pick-up. It might be hot. I don't know what's been happening the last two years. Have you heard anything?"

"Nothing that might connect to you."

"That's good." Jean reached for his cigarettes, and offered one to Dominic, who declined.

"I quit last year."

"So did I," Jean said. "For Lilly, and the family. I bought this pack at the airport before I flew."

"How is that going, Jean? Family life." He had known Jean for years and had yet to adjust to this side of his friend.

77

LaChance lifted his beer and took a drink. His mind leapt back to the island. The vision of Lilly's face swept through his consciousness. She was on the beach, her nude body stretched out on the powdery white sand, which stuck to her thighs and calves, accentuating her tan. For a moment, Jean's eyes glazed over with the dream.

"It's wonderful, more wonderful than I could ever imagine. I'm a father now. Lilly had three kids from before, but she was pregnant when they came to the island. Evie is sixteen months old."

"Wow, good on you, old man," Dominic said. His dark eyes twinkled.

"Yes, it's certainly a different life. Stepping back into the old life at this time will be troubling. I know I'm out of practice with, well, everything." He shook his head quickly. "I need a gun. Can you help me with that?"

"Sure, Jean."

"I need some practice. Feeling a bit, what do they say, rusty?"

"That's what they say."

"I want some sort of disguise. They might know who I am by now. You probably know someone who can change my appearance. I also injured my shoulder recently. Tendons or something. Do you know a doctor who could check it?"

"Sure, I can hook you up. How much time do you have?"

"Not much, I'm afraid. I promised Lilly it would be a quick trip. Besides, I'm anxious to get this behind me."

"How was Lilly with the trip?"

Jean winced at her name. The wounds opened by her fierce words were still deep, sensitive.

"Not good. She was angry when I left. She was right. I couldn't make it better or give her reassurance."

Jean spent the next half hour relaying Hurricane Stephanie's devastation and its effect on their lives, how they needed cash to rebuild, which had brought him back. What he didn't share was his maniacal compulsion to return to his former life.

"I hope it's safe to pick it up," Dominic said.

"Me too. I would like to send it to you right after I visit each bank. There are four banks, so there will be four boxes. I hope to see you again after, but if not, I will send for the money when I return home. Of course, there will be some for you as well."

Death of the Frenchman

"Thank you, but that's not necessary. I'm glad to do it for you. I'll never forget your humanity. You're the only reason I'm still drawing breath."

Unwavering trust defined their relationship. Years before, Jean had warned him in Italy about a revenge hit on his head when one of Dominic's clients was arrested trying to clear customs at an airport.

"I have learned some things in life, my friend." Jean said. "One is that there is nothing more important than a real friend."

"Hear, hear," Dominic said and tipped his glass. Business was concluded.

Long shadows stretched through the garden fence as the sun departed for the day. Soft conversation drifted through the green hideaway. The men laughed about changing diapers and playing games, and Dominic saw that LaChance had found his home. The photo of Lilly and the kids that lived on Jean's person and slept on his nightstand stroked Dominic's heart. Jean's eyes were lit with a fire Dominic had never seen in his friend. LaChance was a man transformed. His eyes swelled when he spoke of Lilly, a grim reminder of their last words. Jean invited him to visit when they rebuilt, and Dominic promised to come. This last opportunity to speak of his family became relaxing escape from the unknown ahead. The next few days would command his being.

Chapter 17

Route 10 carried him mercifully out of the city. Buildings and houses began to disappear and he met fewer and fewer cars until he was alone. The long highway spearing the far horizon felt isolating and strangely, comfortable. The sheer empty beauty of the desert brought an ache to his chest with the memory of his first sight of Lilly.

There was a price to pay for the love of a woman. Before Lilly, he had been Jean LaChance, and only Jean LaChance. Before Lilly, he was able to handle, endure, walk away from anything without a look back. All of that had changed. He was now vulnerable to the emotions that had invaded his life. It was critical to shake that before he arrived in Tucson. If only he could.

He remembered the way of course, and slowed the car as he approached Route 177. The house in the desert was less than twenty miles away, and a visit would only cost him a couple of hours. The surface of the dirt road would tell him if anyone lived there, in which case he'd turn around. Even with the detour, he could make Tucson by nightfall, or stay somewhere on the road. Without knowing why, he needed to go there, to the place where he had fallen in love with Lilly.

He turned north on Route 177, and the two-lane road drew him toward his mark. Visions charged with sexual energy flew through his mind; the shy beautiful woman—nights on the porch—the warm fleshy red wine. Amazingly, it was the same time of year, so the landscape was unchanged.

At mile marker 256, he pulled the car to the left side of the highway and got out to examine the dirt track. The track seemed narrower than he remembered. Desert brush encroached from the sides; Mother Nature reclaiming her custody. The ground was undisturbed and berms of sand had begun to form across the track. No one had been there in a long time.

He stood, tipped his head, and inhaled the hot desert air. The olfactory memory of the vegetation quickened his heart. Eagerness drove him back to the car, and he turned down the road in the direction of the house.

The bad road was worse than before, and the mile to the house, endless. When he rounded the last corner, he stopped immediately as he had done two years before. Nothing had changed. He could almost see ten-year-old Henry rounding the corner with the Winchester .22 gripped in one hand. His first view of Lilly had been from right here. He sucked in a deep breath and drove to the front porch.

Apart from the periodic peeps of desert birds, it was as still as a graveyard. His footfalls were surprisingly loud on the soft sand. LaChance stepped up on the porch and opened the screen door. Oddly, the inner door was locked, but he opened it with the lock pick as if it were the right key.

The scratching of scurrying claws accompanied the creak of the door. The stench of ammonia clung to the dry stale air. The kitchen had been left untouched. Five chairs stood askew around the wooden table. The surface was laced with tiny animal tracks and droppings. Dusty cookware sat on the shelves where Lilly had left it. LaChance glanced into the narrow living room where he had slept and continued through the kitchen and up the stairs. He checked the kids' rooms, which still contained some clothes and a few toys. The beds were torn apart, most likely by the cops who would have searched the house. He crossed the hall to Lilly's bedroom door and stood for a moment before pushing it open.

The room had been tossed. Clothing, sheets, pillows and shoes lay in disarray on the floor. LaChance went to the closet and fingered the few articles of Lilly's clothing dangling from tired wire hangers. He pulled out a blue blouse, held it to his face and closed his eyes. Even after two years, her scent filled his nostrils. He folded the small blouse and shoved it into his front pocket. It was as close as he could keep Lilly for now. He turned toward the bed. The mattress had been lifted and dropped to the side, where it lay partly on the frame and slumped onto the floor. He grabbed the corner of the mattress to throw it on the bedframe, and a jolt of pain shot through his shoulder. He cursed, lay down and closed his eyes.

Evie might have been conceived here. The image of Lilly's nude figure overtook his psyche and he felt his body stir. Her presence was powerful in this room and created a warm, rhythmic flush throughout his body. The four magic days he had spent in this house rewound in his mind: shooting gophers with Henry, repairing the leak in the roof, eating with the family around the kitchen table, drinking wine with Lilly on the porch late at night, and finally, finally making

Death of the Frenchman

love with her for the first time on this very bed. It was the beginning of his present life, and the end of his former life of crime.

But, something else had happened here.

Dewey Jensen was killed in this house, and no one but Jean and Lilly knew the killer. The shooting had been unexpected and violent, spattering dark blood over crumbling linoleum. LaChance had talked to Henry only once about Dewey's death. Henry pretended well. He had hated Dewey, had been protecting his mother. Jean had told Henry it was his only option to ease the boy's ten-year-old mind, but the guilt of parental oversight ate at Jean's stomach. He vowed to address it when he got back to the island.

His mind swam with the breadth of time and events since they had met here. How he had changed in two short years.

LaChance suddenly understood why he was here. This was the close of the episode. It had to close for him to go on. The doubt crippling his confidence had to end at this house. He must expunge Pierre LaPorte; husband, father, businessman, and once again resurrect Jean LaChance; notorious, successful, skilled thief. He had been that man for decades. There had to be a way back.

He took a deep breath and held it captive. Minutes ticked by. His chest and head pounded and swelled with deprivation and launched his mind. Images of France began like a movie in his brain. Visions of all the jobs he had pulled accelerated in sequence from his subconscious. Doors and safes flew open, escape was effortless, complex plots and strategies came back in frames spliced together in a furious assault on his senses. He was invisible. Always armed and potentially dangerous, he feared nothing and no one. He controlled his environment and knew all the exits. He saw his fingers working the most intricate combinations. He traveled swiftly; silently. He was invincible. He was alone.

It was like an acid trip. The experience was surreal, and LaChance had no way of tracking the time frame. It might have been ten minutes or two hours. Images came and went, flashing in related sequences. Deep breathing provided the sound track. Snippets of French conversation narrated the film, which included faces he had not seen in many years.

Abruptly, the vision stopped, and LaChance opened his eyes. He got up from the bed and crossed the room to the mirror above the bureau. The man staring back was Jean LaChance.

He was ready.

He drew the blouse from his pocket, folded it neatly, and deposited it on the bureau. Next came the photo of Lilly and the kids, which he laid gently on the blouse. Without another glance at either, LaChance left the room, closing the door behind him. He descended the stairs, and with eyes fixed straight ahead, walked through the front door, got in his car and drove away from the house in the desert for the last time.

Chapter 18

Santino was now familiar with the perfect lattice pattern of Tucson. This morning's phone call had provided the day's schedule. An officer at a large downtown bank had recognized LaChance from the photo. Santino had a three o'clock interview.

Thomas Hutchins greeted Santino at the service desk and escorted him to a large glass conference room complete with gigantic walnut table. A plump, pleasant-looking woman of about forty was sitting at the table alone, looking like a kid in detention. Her clenched fingers were wrung white. President Hutchins introduced her as Patty.

"Hello, Patty," Santino said, smiling. His skin twitched with excitement. She was the second person he had met to have spoken with Jean LaChance. The first had been Lilly.

"Hello," Patty said. Her folded hands were in constant motion. She untangled them clumsily and shook his.

"I'm Private Investigator Guy Santino. I'd like to ask you a few questions."

"Wow, an Investigator? I have to let you know, I'm really nervous. What is this about? I've never been involved in anything like this before."

"Please relax Patty. You're actually quite essential to my investigation. Please call me Guy."

"Alright . . . Guy. Is this connected with the photograph of Mr. Smith?"

Smith, thought Santino. He had a name.

Santino drew a copy of the photo out of an envelope and placed it on the table in front of Patty.

"Is this the man?" he asked.

"Yes, well, I'm pretty sure it is. It was a long time ago. Mr. Hutchins says it's been two years. For one thing, I think he was much older than the man in that photo."

"The photo was taken thirty years ago."

"Oh!" She paused. "Yes, then, I believe it's the same man."

"Can you recall any of the conversation that day?"

"Well, Mr. Smith—David, he said to call him—wanted to rent a safe-deposit box. He needed a large one, but he didn't have an account with us, so I told him he could open an account, then he would be able to rent the box. That's our policy, you know."

"And did he open an account?"

"Yes, he did. He was very nice, and oh! He had all the numbers memorized. He said he never had to write anything down. That part was really memorable. I was impressed."

"How long was he here?"

"Let's see . . . I guess it must have been about twenty minutes, maybe a half hour."

"Were you talking with him the entire time?"

"Yes, the manager took his paperwork and I sat at the desk with Mr. Smith."

"What did you talk about?"

"Oh, the usual things. The weather, Tucson, traveling."

"Did he say where he was from?"

"No, he didn't. He didn't really talk a lot. He just answered the usual questions and filled out the papers, and then he went into the box, and then, well, then he left."

"Did you notice an accent?"

"An accent?" Patty's brow crumpled and her lips pursed up tight. "No, no I don't think so. He had a very . . . normal voice. I think he was from out-of-state. I do remember, he gave an address in California."

"Do we have that address on record?" Santino directed the question to President Hutchins.

"I believe it's on his application. But that's restricted information, Mr. Santino. For the security of our customers, we can't release that."

Damn, thought Santino. Of course. Another policy to jam up his operation. Though it was likely the address would lead him to an empty lot or abandoned building, just for fun.

Death of the Frenchman

Santino continued with more questions, a few which couldn't be answered because of their privacy policy, and he learned nothing further about David Smith, the man with a photographic memory. He requested a call if contact was made and left his card with President Hutchins.

A blast of sizzling street air hit his face as he pushed out the glass doors. He was starving. The trip to Tucson had been last minute, and he hadn't bothered to stop. A Mexican restaurant stood not too far from the bank on the same street, and the familiar aromas filled his mouth with saliva. Santino ordered beef and green chili enchiladas and took out his notebook.

He enjoyed the jitter of the chase. He now had an individual who had spoken with the man during the same time Santino had been in pursuit. They had prints on record that could be matched, should there be another opportunity for LaChance to surface.

Which, of course, was the hitch.

LaChance had disappeared two years before, presumably from the airport in Tucson, and Lilly had disappeared seven months later. They knew they were suspects in the Richard Prescott robbery and possibly in the death of Dewey Jensen, and would act accordingly; change their identity at the very least, or quit the country for an innocuous, anonymous lifestyle. There were too many variables. Apart from supplying all the banks in Tucson with the name David Smith, there was little else to do but simply wait for LaChance to break the surface. Santino was at a momentary dead end.

He could, of course, pass the information along to the LAPD, who could issue a warrant for the safe-deposit boxes. Santino considered this. That would mean he would lose control of this case. His ego wasn't quite ready to relinquish control.

He munched on his enchiladas and added Patty's contribution to the notes. Good girl, he thought. But the page held too many question marks. His knee bounced enough to shake the table. Nowhere to go for now. He had to let it go and move onto other cases until he heard anything further.

He finished his meal, paid the check and returned to his car for the trip back to L.A. The day was still horribly hot, and summer was still winding up.

Chapter 19

LaChance arrived in Tucson shortly after dark. On the way into the city, he stopped at an office supply store and purchased four medium-sized boxes, packing tape and paper. He checked into a hotel centrally located to the banks he would visit the next day. The long ride had stiffened his body. He needed to walk.

As he stepped onto the street, the warm desert breeze hit his face, bringing with it reminiscent scents of victory. The last time he had encountered those same aromas was the day he had hidden the cash stolen from Richard Prescott's house. Tomorrow, he would collect the money and leave immediately for L.A. With luck, he would be flying back to Caracas within a week. Dominic would have his new identification. He would discard the documents he used to rent the safe-deposit boxes. Any dumpster on the outskirts of Tucson would do.

Dominic had gotten a gun for him—a Glock 9mm identical to the one he had carried two years before. The weight was familiar in his hand. He had stopped along the road from L.A. and found a secluded spot away from the highway to practice loading and firing the weapon. He was thankful that the injured shoulder wasn't connected to his shooting arm. One magazine of shells was sufficient to check his aim. Funny, how some things never went away.

LaChance found a restaurant and sat down to eat. Dinner was palatable, but he wasn't eating for pleasure. He used this last opportunity to think about Lilly and the kids. By this time, they would be in bed or reading a story. He wished for a second that he had the photo, then shoved it from his mind. Distractions were dangerous. He needed all of his wits.

Two years was more than enough time for law enforcement to follow up on the trail of Jean LaChance. Sooner or later, they could discover his identity. The Frenchman respected the men who enforced laws. It was the essence of survival. He was in the advantage, and the time that had elapsed was partly in his favor.

Even if they knew his identity, the bank safe-deposit boxes had been rented under a different name. Banks conducted thousands of transactions every day, and records tended to move slowly in every system he had encountered. There was also a chance that they hadn't a clue who he was. In that event, there was no danger at all. He wished he felt certain.

When he fled Arizona, cops had brought Lilly to the airport. He marked them as soon as Lilly arrived and warned him with her eyes. He remembered their faces well enough to recognize them again. If he saw those same cops, he would know. But what were the odds of that? They hadn't identified him at the time, or he would've been caught. If they had identified him since then, there was a chance the FBI was involved, which would mean trouble. FBI agents were competent; well-trained, intelligent, educated. But it would give him one edge. The nearest field office was in Phoenix, over a hundred miles away. Even if they flew, by the time someone could be alerted and travel to Tucson, his errand would be complete. His biggest advantage was the element of surprise. No one knew he was here.

He would visit all the banks in quick succession, mailing the boxes with the cash after each collection to avoid carrying money. There were post office branches close enough to each bank, and the boxes were already addressed. If all went well, he might hang onto the last safe-deposit box stash and carry it with him back to L.A.

The waitress came over to give him his check. Jean smiled and thanked her, then took the time to chat about the restaurant and the food. The waitress was a nice, pretty brunette, and flirted a bit for a bigger tip. Jean was proud of his polished American accent. All the time spent with Lilly and the kids had been useful in that regard.

Lilly.

Was she still angry? LaChance doubted it. He knew her well enough by now. She was emotional, but she was also strong and smart. She would feel guilty about his last moments there. He felt guilty. Her words had wounded him, but he knew they were driven by fear. He had already forgiven her. It would all be fine in a couple of days.

Lilly Parsons had given him life in the form of love and four children. Before Lilly, his existence had been mechanical—a robot carrying out automatic tasks in a meaningless daily grind. He had no one, thought about no one, talked to almost no one about anything significant. Crime had been his life, and had served him well for many years. He had never been lonely, had never thought about loneliness one way or another. The minutia of his profession had filled every moment of every day.

Lilly was life itself. From the first moment they met, LaChance had felt an alien emotion that was simultaneously wonderful and terrifying. Before Lilly, women had merely been a means of physical satisfaction—a pleasurable diversion. Other than that, he had nothing at all to do with them. Lilly had opened the mysteries of humanity. She had given him the gifts of trust, love and devotion, aspects of life that had become ultimately important in the past two years. Things he had never imagined.

LaChance saw people now. He saw them as husbands and wives, children, parents, uncles, aunts, friends, lovers. He knew the love and dependence of children. And the first time he held Constance Evelyn LaPorte, he had wept uncontrollably.

Evie had been born in the nearest hospital on a neighboring island. As soon as Lilly had gone into labor, the two of them jumped on a plane and left, with Henry in charge at home. Jean had been nervous. Lilly was as cool as a clam. With three births already behind her, she knew exactly what to do and bore the pain well. It was LaChance's first witness to the birth of a human being. He watched weak-kneed as the baby's head crowned, and then popped out from between Lilly's legs. Evie slid into the world with a wail she would carry from that moment forward. The doctor placed the baby on Lilly's stomach.

LaChance was frozen. He watched from the side as Lilly laughed and cooed sobs of release and ecstasy, counting the infant's fingers and toes, turning her to inspect her completeness. The nurses chattered non-stop and fussed over the baby with feminine efficiency. They wrapped Evie in a soft towel after a gentle sponge bath. One nurse turned around to LaChance and offered his daughter to him.

He had never before held a baby. She was so little, even his skilled hands were afraid of dropping her. The nurse laughed without judgment, then pushed the baby tenderly into his arms, instructing in soft Spanish how to hold her. LaChance stared down at the little creature—his daughter. He glanced up at Lilly, who lay on the bed with a wet smile.

"That's your daughter," Lilly whispered.

"Yeah," LaChance managed. He looked back down at the baby. The tears came with no warning. He stood helplessly at the end of the bed feeling his temperature rise. The nurse guided him to the side of the bed, where he reclined next to Lilly with the precious infant between them. He was dumbstruck. He touched the baby's face with a large finger and kissed Lilly gently on the forehead.

Lilly lay next to him, watching his eyes experience the creation of a human being. Memories of Henry's birth flashed through her mind. Jean's hands and lips trembled and attempted to gain control. She stroked his temple.

"It's amazing, isn't it?" she said.

Jean nodded his head rapidly, unable to produce any words. Unrelenting tears drained down to his chin. He would never be the same.

The kids were wild with excitement when they returned to the island two days later. Sherri stood over Evie and giggled a steady nervous stream. The boys stood behind and called her name again and again, then broke into peals of laughter when she opened her eyes.

Lilly relaxed into full-time mothering for the first time. She had been busier with the other kids, who were now old enough to take care of themselves. Jean allowed her to—demanded—that she do nothing more. He stayed close to home and checked on them every half hour during the day. He learned how to care for the delicate baby and soon was diapering like a pro. But he most liked it when Lilly nursed the baby, and would sit for entire feedings watching them. Lilly was exhausted and rested most of the day, but at night, he would arouse her with caresses, sending her into orgasms that required every ounce of residual energy. She finally had to beg him to stop, but he was wildly aroused by the new mother, as horny as a teenage boy. He waited with agonizing patience until she was again ready for intercourse and then had to be careful not to hurt her as his wanton spirit drove his love into the mother of his child.

The other children became invisible for a time, and Henry roamed farther and farther from the guest house, exploring the island and establishing a reputation among the villagers as a competent helper. He went out in boats with some of the locals and became skillful at hauling in fish to sell at the markets. At the end of many days, he thumped a thirty pound bass up the back steps into the kitchen. Both of his parents were impressed. Henry was once again the family hunter.

Amos and Sherri helped their father with the guest house chores, and he made time to spend with them, playing or walking after work. It was the best time of all of their lives.

"Can I get you anything else sir?"

LaChance's eyes were glazed over with the daydream. He politely declined, and forced his mind back to Tucson, draining the last of the wine from his glass before rising to leave. Losing himself in thoughts of Lilly and his family had let the loneliness back in, but tomorrow he would chase them from his head and focus on the money retrieval. He had a few things to complete before he could lie down and rest well.

As he stepped onto the street, he looked across at the first bank on his list.

Chapter 20

Street light flooded in through a split in the window curtain. The city was still dark; the streets, quiet. Perfect. Plenty of time to fully awake, eat a big, meat-heavy breakfast that would hold off another meal until after his bank crawl was complete. He rang room service and showered.

Fast work was safest. The less time between banks, the better his chances. Even with an identity, authorities couldn't know for certain which banks held his rented safe-deposit boxes until he actually arrived to empty them. A friend of Dominic's who worked as a movie make-up artist had created a disguise that changed his appearance and aged him substantially. Sprigs of wiry gray hair poked out from below the rim of a worn fedora. The "new" nose was bulbous and showed telltale spider veins of heavy drinking. Age spots adorned his face and neck. Though there was a resemblance to the former David Smith, mostly in the eyes, it effectively concealed his real face. Dominic then took photos of Jean and renewed David Smith driver's license. David Smith held the keys to the safe-deposit boxes. Even if the new photo did not exactly match the photo on the old license, the name and numbers were identical. Bank officers would likely not check, as long as everything matched.

LaChance let himself out a hotel side door, went to the rental car and left all of his tools, including the keys to the car, inside, and the vehicle unlocked. He carried a large, square bag with a plastic garbage bag inside for the cash. Just after eight thirty in the morning, his heart beating steadily, Jean LaChance, a.k.a David Smith, pulled opened the door to the Arizona Federal Bank.

This early in the day, few customers were inside, and LaChance accessed an officer immediately. A pleasant young woman waited on him. The age difference was advantageous, and she 'yes sir, no sir-ed' him into the vault and put in his key, followed by hers before sliding out the large box and placing it gently on a table.

She excused herself, and LaChance waited until she had exited the vault, then opened the box. The sight of stacks of cash neatly piled to the top of the box increased the pace of his heart. He shook out the plastic bag and threw handful after handful of the bundles in, then deposited the entire bag into his duffle, zipped it up and exited the vault door, left slightly ajar by the officer. She smiled and thanked him and he exited out on to the street, forcing his pace to a slow lumber. He drove three blocks, parked alongside a quiet street, withdrew the money, carefully rolling the cash in plastic wrap, then in aluminum foil to reduce x-ray possibility and mask the smell that money always carried. The neat packets then went into one of his packing boxes, and he stuffed the empty space with paper and taped the box shut. He threw the box on the passenger's seat and drove to the nearest post office.

He insured the box for five thousand dollars and glanced at his watch. The whole thing had taken less than an hour. Beautiful. At this rate, allowing for travel time between banks and post offices, he would be finished by early afternoon, when he would turn the car in the direction of Los Angeles.

The second bank took longer. More customers were filing in, and he was forced to wait in line for an officer. Everything went just as it had the first time, and again, he found a post office and sent off the box of cash to Dominic's address. Confidence returned. The third bank proceeded just as smoothly, and at one o'clock, he searched for a parking space without success on the street in front of the First National Bank of Tucson. Finally, he gave up and drove into a parking garage.

LaChance didn't like garages. The single entrance/exit was designed like a trap. The second and third banks had been busy, and traffic was heavy. Too much time had elapsed. David Smith had already made three bank transactions today involving large safe-deposit boxes. There was a definite pattern. The cardinal rule of illicit activity—no patterns.

His apprehension was mounting with every passing minute, and he breathed deeply and told himself that everything was fine. Walking from the garage to the bank, a pang of fear caught in his throat, but he dismissed it as nerves. He was anxious to have this part of his day behind him.

He stopped on the sidewalk outside the bank. The oppressive sun baked his skin. Creepy anxiety crept up his scalp. He hesitated, and turned to walk away. Then he remembered.

Of course.

Death of the Frenchman

This was the bank where he was required to open an account and spoke with the officer named Patty, wasn't it? It was the longest contact he had made the day he stashed the money from the heist before leaving Tucson. He would have to watch for her. He certainly didn't want the same officer. She might remember him. She had even said I'll remember you next time. His face was so altered, she might be suspicious.

Of course. That's all it was. LaChance pulled open the door and entered the bank.

He glanced around at the desks, not finding Patty at first. He stood at the counter with the blank deposit slips and continued to search. Then he spied her, down at the end of the row of desks. He went to the opposite end and sat in a chair to wait for an officer. He was called after several minutes. At the desk, he made his request and produced identification. The officer seemed to react normally, business as usual. In ten minutes, the whole episode would be behind him.

They walked together to the vault. He handed her his key and waited for her to open the door. The officer stepped outside after depositing the box on a table.

The click of the heavy door made his eyebrows jump. Typically, the door was closed to a crack to provide privacy for the customer without locking them inside. Instant panic filled his chest and quickened his breath. He looked at the door and listened hard. He strained his ears through the heavy silence of the vault. He lifted the lid of the safe-deposit box and filled his bag with the last of Prescott's money, then went to the door and listened. Nothing. He knocked lightly on the door, and when there was no response, pounded harder with his fist. Maybe it was just a mistake. But something was not right.

Shadows of Lilly skittered through his mind.

He heard metallic sounds, and the vault door cracked open a few inches. He breathed easier. It was just a mistake. But the door didn't open any farther. LaChance peered through the crack and saw part of a black uniform just outside the door. It couldn't be. They were cops.

Someone outside the door started to say something that began with "Mr. Smith," but LaChance heaved his weight against the heavy door, flinging it open. Six or seven police officers surrounded him instantly. He took out the first two with the door and made it past two more with his momentum, but a sudden sharp pain shot down his spine, and everything went black.

Chapter 21

"Jean LaChance."

The dream of Lilly's smiling face blurred, then pulsated, then retreated from his subconscious like water going down a drain. The sound of his name brought consciousness. LaChance shook his head slowly and winced at the screaming pain pounding his skull. He opened his eyes and caught sight of bright orange. He blinked hard and then realized it was his clothing. He was wearing an orange jump suit.

Where was he? Suddenly he remembered; the bank, the cops. The far side of the room loomed into focus. A man with a vaguely familiar face stood on the far side of vertical bars.

Jesus. He was in a cell. He sat up slowly.

"Mr. LaChance, my name is Guy Santino. You're a hard guy to catch up with."

Guy Santino. Did the name mean anything?

"I've been following your case—the robbery case—Richard Prescott of Los Angeles. Remember? You were picked up at the bank retrieving the cash you stole two years ago with Dewey Jensen. Remember Dewey? Ol' dead Dewey in the desert? I've got some questions for you, LaChance."

Jean dropped his head into his hands. His shoulder and the back of his head were in agony. This guy had been following him for two years? Then he remembered; the airport. When Lilly had warned him at the airport, there had been two cops looking for Lilly's accomplice. The Hispanic man who was searching the crowd. The seasoned cop. Right now he was standing outside the cell that held LaChance prisoner.

LaChance said nothing. Santino reached into his pocket and pulled out a pack of Camels.

He gestured with the pack and LaChance nodded. Santino produced a lighter. It was Jean's. He lit the cigarette in his mouth and threw it between the bars, where it landed on the cement floor. LaChance picked it slowly off the floor and took a long drag. His eyes followed the smoke upward to Santino's face. He nodded his head once in acknowledgement.

"I have to say, you could be in some hot water. The FBI is very interested in your whereabouts, LaChance. Unlawful flight to avoid prosecution. Sound familiar? Seems the French police would like to see you, too. Me? I'm impressed. You're an escape artist. The Paris police confirm that. That was quite an exit from Lilly's house in California. We put an APB out on the LeSabre, but never found it. That's like a magic trick out there in the middle of nowhere with that big shiny car."

He paused to let reality sink in. LaChance sat smoking; no reaction whatsoever.

"I know you're not going to tell me anything. I'm just introducing myself, and I probably won't see you much after today. You'll be doing a lot of traveling in the next couple of days. It'll be good to get back to France, eh?"

Santino paused again, hoping his words would carry some impact. Prison had a way of reducing men. Even behind the bars, dressed in the neon prison clothes, the prisoner looked lethal. This man was larger than life, despite his present situation. LaChance held Santino's eyes with a steady gaze, neither vengeful nor fearful. It was mechanical, inhuman. The air between them was charged with electricity that threatened to melt the bars away. Santino had to break the hold with conversation.

"Where's Lilly Parsons?" Santino asked.

Lilly. His sweet wife, his daughter Evie's mother. Her worst fear had come true. There was no way of contacting her, even if they gave him access to a phone. Suffocating grief gripped LaChance's chest. She was right. He shouldn't have risked it. On the outside, he showed no reaction to the name. He stared at Santino without expression. Fuck you, he thought. You'll never find Lilly.

"Alright, LaChance. I've enjoyed our conversation. Early tomorrow morning, the FBI field guys will be here from Phoenix. I'm sure they'll have lots of questions for you."

In a gesture of kindness, Santino pulled an ice pack from his coat pocket and shook it before throwing it between the black bars.

"I'll try to get someone to look at your head. They whacked you pretty good."

Death of the Frenchman

Jean felt the back of his head, crusty with dried blood where the club had hit home. He again nodded, but said nothing. Santino waited for a few more minutes, but it was obvious the man didn't plan to speak to him.

Santino was disappointed. He would love to hear the man speak. In a twisted way, he respected LaChance deeply. A life underground is a tough existence. Its residents are loyal and devoted to the few they trust. LaChance would never admit to knowing Lilly Parsons. Santino felt a twinge of envy. The Inspector was intimidated by the man trapped in the cell. He was thankful for the bars, knowing he would be no match for the Frenchman, armed or otherwise. He turned to go.

"What time is it?" LaChance asked.

The sudden question startled Santino. He glanced at his watch.

"It's 7:10."

Just after seven in the evening. Lilly and the kids would be eating dinner about now. They would laugh at Evie playing with her food, and try to get her to put it in her mouth instead of on the ground. Perhaps before, they had walked to the beach, where the evening sand still held the warmth of the day's sun, splash in the water and chase the gulls. Evie would point at different things and try to call their names. Just the vision of his little family brought tears to his eyes.

"Thank you," the prisoner said, and turned his back on Santino to lie down.

Santino exited the door to the holding tank. He would return in the morning to watch the process. Though he hadn't actually collared LaChance, he was the reason the man was locked up, and felt strangely bad. They had recovered just over one hundred thousand dollars in cash from the last safe-deposit box, but nothing more. LaChance hadn't been carrying anything else but the identification necessary to access the box. No keys, no weapon, no money. He was good. There might be a car parked somewhere containing the balance of the heist, but it would take a while to find it. They were just beginning to sort out the case of French thief Jean LaChance.

Back in his cell, Jean held the ice to the back of his head and tried to relax. He shamed himself again and again. He should have followed his instincts. Twice before entering the bank, fear had gripped him. He'd be half way to Los Angeles right now if he hadn't carried through for the lousy few bills in the last bank. It had been stupid. Egotistical. What the hell at this point was he trying to prove? And now he was behind bars.

He looked around the cell. He had only hours before the FBI was scheduled to arrive. He had to get out of here by morning. After that, his chances of escape were negligible.

He guessed the cell was housed in a holding tank somewhere in Tucson. He had been unconscious for the ride from the bank, so he wasn't sure how far or where he was. The cell was built well. There was no way of breaking out. He would have to find another way, and he had to do it by morning.

Lilly's last words echoed in his throbbing head.

We have no way of knowing if anyone is there laying a trap for you, and if they catch you, I'll never know. You'll simply disappear. And I'll be here with the kids alone and we'll never hear from you again.

He had to get out.

Chapter 22

Lilly cleaned up the last of the lunch. She finished by wiping the top of the table and hanging the dish cloth up to dry.

Amos and Sherri had taken the baby outside, where she could hear them playing with a friendly stray dog that had appeared after Stephanie. No one seemed to know where he had come from, but the dog showed up every day at mealtime and hung around for scraps. Lilly had started to call the dog 'Scraps,' and it stuck. He was a sweet little dog that loved the kids and stuck to them like a magnet. As the days went by, Lilly began to realize they had a new pet.

She glanced at the calendar suspended from the tent upright. It had been well over a week since Jean's departure. What did that mean? Two days to get to the States, a couple of days to get ready for the bank transactions. Lilly wondered what that might involve. He must have a contact of some kind somewhere. He had never told her. Was he carrying a gun? Probably. She shuddered suddenly without knowing why. He had been armed when they met. It was a lethal looking handgun of some kind. She remembered how dangerous he looked with the gun in his hand.

The last two years had flown. Periodically, she allowed herself to ponder who Jean might have been before they met. Every time that sensation arose, she shoved the feeling aside. It was simply too dangerous to think about, and, hell, it was history. Jean was now her husband, the devoted father of Evie and three children who were not his own. He was not that former person anymore. Not the person she had first encountered on a lonely, deserted road in California desert when she had been at the end of the line with three kids and no way out.

He might already be in Tucson. He might be done with the banks, loaded with money and on his way back home right now. She wouldn't know until he poked his head into their tent with his beautiful, shy smile. Her heart ached.

The kids had been brilliant during his absence. Amos had taken full charge of the baby, because Lilly was saddled with the grind of daily chores without the benefit of electricity. Ramón stopped by every morning to check on them and relay any new information. She felt safe, even with Jean in the States. Their present home had canvas sides, but it was comfortable. Jean had left them well set. He had made sure of the tent, the generator, the stove, the clothes line, the beds. She shook her head. There was no victory in guilt.

The day hung before her with mountains of chores, but she felt like being a Real Mom today. Maybe they could go swimming or take a walk to see how everyone else was faring. The community was all in the same condition. It was time to reconnect with island friends.

A sudden attack of dread swept through her, like a rogue wave crashing onto shore. She almost had to sit down. She glanced at the clock. One thirty in the afternoon. What was it? She shook her head and tried to focus.

The kids.

She threw open the tent flap, her eyes darting back and forth down the sandy street. All three were sitting on the ground across the road playing with a hermit crab.

But the feeling was overwhelming. Tears squeezed their way out of her eyes.

Maybe this was something that came with recent childbirth, only it had been sixteen months. There had been no postpartum depression associated with Evie's birth, not like the others, when her marriage to John Parsons had been falling apart from the moment they spoke their vows. Whatever it was, the feeling was horrific.

Lilly pushed it away, but the creeping sensation that it was somehow connected to Jean frightened her. She took a deep breath and reached for a backpack. Some snacks and a bottle of water, a diaper for the baby and the current dog-eared paperback all went inside. Lilly left the tent and called for the kids. They would spend the afternoon on the beach in the sunshine. Scraps would accompany them. Supper was still hours away and life was good.

Life was good. The afternoon was almost perfect, except that Dad was missing. The kids played in the mild surf, laughing and filling their clothes with the ubiquitous sand that would require drying first on the clothes line, then shaking out, then washing by hand, then drying again, but Lilly didn't care. On the island, they didn't even have swim suits. They swam in their clothes and dealt with it later.

Sherri suddenly pounced on the blanket and sprayed Lilly with water. Her curly hair was matted flat on her forehead.

"Mommy, come swimming with us!"

"That's okay, honey. I think I'll just sit here today."

"Awww, come on!"

"No, Sherri, I just want to sit here, I said." Her tone was harsher than she intended.

Sherri pouted visibly, then jumped to her feet and wrapped her chubby arms around her mother.

"Mommy, Daddy'll come home soon. Promise." She raced back toward the water where Amos was sitting with Evie. Lilly's nose reddened and she blinked back tears. Even Sherri was dealing better than she was.

The lazy afternoon stretched out into peaceful, slow playtime resembling something like normal life. They played, laughed and ate and pretended that everything was status quo. They all were good at normal. It was the farthest thing from any of their experiences, so normal was easy to achieve.

The panicky sensation stayed with Lilly for the rest of the day and into the night. There was no way to form a context. Had she known that Jean was locked up in a holding cell in Tucson, she would've been terrified.

Death of the Frenchman

Chapter 23

The minutes raced through the night, but LaChance had no way of tracking time. He was the only prisoner in the cell block. He could see the steel door through which Santino had come. A small high window with reinforced glass was built into the door.

That was the way out. The rest of the short hallway held additional cells and ended in a solid cement wall. He had searched every inch of his enclosure and found no reasonable escape route. No one else had come through the door since Santino's visit.

He didn't dare sleep. He simply had to wait for an opportunity.

That opportunity came around 2:00 a.m. The outside door opened, and a young officer stepped into the hallway. He was dressed in full police uniform, complete with shiny badge, gun in holster, not a crease in sight. He stopped in front of the cell. "Knowles" shone from his silver nametag.

"Are you hungry, man?" the officer asked.

He looked about fourteen. Beautiful. Rookie meets pro. He had never before met a man like Jean LaChance. LaChance shook his head and rubbed the back of his neck in apparent pain. He needed to look old, injured, vulnerable.

"I could use something to drink."

"What do you want; coffee, water?"

Jean poured on the foreign accent. Impress the greenhorn.

"Water would be just fine, unless you have a bottle of Cabernet Sauvignon out there."

The young officer laughed. His demeanor implied respect. Undoubtedly, all the cops in this precinct had heard about LaChance's reputation. The FBI. That was big. Any prisoner who warranted the arrival of the FBI was a criminal with a substantial history. Though they would never admit it, every one of them drooled for a conversation with the infamous Jean LaChance, a prisoner with an international reputation.

LaChance smiled. This was good. Talk to the kid. Make a joke. Let him feel close. Let him see the prisoner in pain.

The officer produced a key ring and opened the outer door. LaChance watched him. He disappeared for several minutes, and returned with a paper cup. The door automatically swung shut behind him with a clunk.

Good. No one would hear them.

LaChance was sitting on the edge of the bed with his head down, his right hand still on the back of his neck.

Come closer, young one.

Officer Knowles had learned in the academy classroom never to approach the bars of a cell holding a potentially dangerous criminal. He had also never been in that situation before. His attention was focused on the famous thief in the cell, who was apparently in a lot of pain from the blow to the head at the bank. The prisoner was looking down. Dried blood clumped in his hair.

Officer Knowles stood just outside the bars and offered the cup.

"Here you go, man."

In one motion, LaChance grabbed the hand holding the cup and pulled with all his weight, smashing the young man against the bars face-first. A shout that might have come out of the cop's mouth was stifled by the grip LaChance had on his throat, choking off any sound and cutting off the officer's air.

The water spun to the floor. Their faces were inches apart. The young officer's eyes were frozen in panic. He had fucked up, and the expression on LaChance's face confirmed it. As life-sustaining oxygen drained from his brain, accelerated by panic, the lights slowly dimmed, and Officer Knowles slumped to the floor outside the bars, guided down safely, gently by the prisoner.

LaChance reached outside the bars and rolled the man over. A bolt of lightning shot through his shoulder. He ignored it. He found the ring of keys and pulled them inside the cell, searching for the key that might open his cell door. The second key he tried clicked in the lock, and one push swung the door open. He dragged the kid inside and stripped off his shirt. The officer was not a small man, but LaChance was taller. It would be a tight fit, but far less conspicuous than the orange jumpsuit.

He pulled on the uniform shirt and forced the buttons together. He took the gun from the cop's holster, then stripped off the man's pants and pulled them on. He shoved the gun in the right front pant pocket and tucked in the shirt. He pocketed the keys. Stepping outside the cell door, he closed it quietly behind him and locked it. The uniform would buy him time, but only seconds. LaChance had not regained consciousness after his capture until he was in the cell, so he had no way of knowing the layout of the police station. He crept low to the door and peered out the reinforced glass.

A desk stood to the left with an officer behind it. The clock on the wall told him it was 2:10 a.m.

Perfect. It wouldn't be light for four hours. Stairs leading down to the right probably went to the front of the station, but he couldn't know that, and besides, he would have to pass directly in front of the officer seated at the desk.

No one else was around.

LaChance leaned back and looked through the glass to the right, opposite the desk. There was a door, identical to this one, with a light on the other side. What did that mean? Was it a bathroom? Stairs? He had no way of knowing, but that was where he was going. He leaned forward again and watched the officer at the desk. All he needed was a couple of seconds. Turn your head. Go get a cup of coffee.

LaChance pulled the keys from his pocket and flipped through them until one turned the tumbler. He stood motionless on the cell side of the door for long minutes watching the officer, his muscles tight with anticipation. Nothing went through his head. He waited for the man to move.

Suddenly, the officer said, "What?" and turned his head to someone behind him. He got up from the chair and disappeared from view.

LaChance exited the door quickly with his back to the desk and reached for the other door knob. It turned like magic in his hand and he was through in a fraction of a second. He couldn't know if the officer at the desk had seen him, but now the clock was ticking. They would discover his escape at any second. Behind the door, stairs led down two short flights to a lower level. Dim lights illuminated a hall with lockers, a janitor closet and storage.

Please, please, he thought. Just give me a way out.

At the end of the hall, the passageway went right. Rounding the corner, he collided with a uniformed officer, who was more surprised than LaChance. A panicked cry escaped the cop's mouth, as LaChance's muscle memory drove a commanding leg sweep that catapulted the officer against the wall. LaChance jumped on the stunned man and repeated his choke-hold, putting the man out in seconds. He released the cop and listened carefully for any indication he had been detected. The hallway ended at a solid metal door, barely visible in the dim light.

The door was likely alarmed. He tried the knob. As he expected, it was locked. He turned back to the unconscious officer and found a set of keys clipped to the cop's belt. One at a time, he flipped through the keys and tried them all in the lock. The sweat streamed down his face and burned his eyes. There were just too many keys, and he might be discovered at any second. One big silver key went in upside-down and he cursed and turned it around. A solid clunk echoed through the hallway. He pressed his face to the window and scanned from left to right, taking in the dark alleyway beyond. Taking a deep breath, he held it lightly and braced himself for the alarm. The door groaned open, and he stepped out into the warm desert breeze. In seconds he was a shadow that disappeared down the alley into the dark streets of Tucson, once again a free man.

Chapter 24

LaChance ran for several blocks, trying to figure out which way was which. His footfalls pounded like shock waves through the desolate neighborhood streets, and he chose grass where he could to silence his frantic flight. The mathematically organized streets of the big city soon provided compass headings, but it was impossible to know which direction to go. As soon as he felt a safe distance from the station, he started checking car doors. The first sixteen were locked, but then an old Buick door opened with a squeal.

LaChance was in and had the car wired in seconds. He tossed the gun on the seat.

He noted the miles on the odometer and pulled onto the street. Driving slowly enough to avoid unwanted attention, he cruised down the street, praying for something familiar. The only place to go was where he had been caught.

He needed the rental car. It was legal. It also held all of his tools, his gun, money, identification and a change of clothes.

The first major street he came to ran north and south. The name was unfamiliar, but he had to keep moving, had to appear just like a normal driver who would know where they were going. His internal compass told him to turn right. The street was deserted. He drove north on the street for about a mile, passing side street after side street until another major intersection appeared ahead.

Broadway. He knew Broadway. It would take him within two blocks of the parking garage.

En route, he spotted a couple of police cars cruising the night shift. No sirens, no lights. That was a good sign. Familiar landmarks started to crop up on either side of the street. Though the distance was only several miles, it seemed to take hours.

He passed the First National Bank on the left. The garage was well lit, with an attendant sitting in the booth bent over a paperback. Her eyes didn't leave the page when he entered.

The rental car was alone on the third level. He parked the stolen vehicle next to it and wiped down the steering wheel with his sleeve out of habit. There was no one around, so he popped the trunk and stripped next to the rental in the shadows.

His own clothes felt comfortable, and certainly less conspicuous than a cop's uniform. He threw the uniform in the trunk, and when he retrieved the keys from under the seat, the sharp rattle made him jump. The jingle echoed against the cement walls of the silent garage. He held up his hands and watched the tremor in disbelief. He needed to relax for just a second.

A pack of cigarettes lay on the console, and he lit up and dropped his head back onto the vinyl headrest. Smoke curled up to the headliner in gray feathers swirling through his heavy exhales.

Adrenalin was still coursing through his entire body. Eerie sensations like tiny electrical shocks fired sporadically in hands, his feet, his neck and hair follicles. The cigarette lifted to his lips was a moving target as he grappled for control.

He had come so close. So close to lifetime confinement. He forced his body to lengthen and deepened his breath. By gripping the steering wheel, he could make himself believe his hands were at rest. This was new. Escape had always been a game he played with panache. For the first time in his fifty years, LaChance was rattled beyond control.

His mind jumped through the bank transaction, the escape, the stolen car sitting next to his rental, Lilly, the kids, the island. Sleep deprivation clouded his brain and robbed his energy. He snapped his head forward and realized he had almost nodded off. He ran his fingers through his hair and shook his head. He had to move.

Now what? Should he take the highway? Would they put up road blocks? Was it too late?

The clock on the dash read 2:46 a.m. He decided to chance it. The highway was the fastest exit.

The parking lot attendant wore a fallow face that barely bothered to look at him as she counted the change and returned to her book. He hoped she hadn't noticed his hands, but pushed it from his mind. Just keep going, he whispered.

The squeal of a siren erupted as he turned onto the street. It quickened his heart. The highway was only minutes away, and by the time he arrived at the on

Death of the Frenchman

ramp, several police cars had passed him, sirens screaming, lights flashing. They were headed the other way.

He checked the gauges on the dash. The tank was full. No sense in stopping any time soon. He would pass through Phoenix before light. California was four hours away.

That's when he would stop.

He switched on the radio and found a 70s station. The music soothed his racing heart. Pushing back into his seat, he slowed his breath to large, long inhales. As each mile passed under the rental's tires, his arms fell onto his lap and he was finally able to consider events over the past twenty-four hours. Sleep was what he needed, would heal him, but the excitement of the dicey escape promised to carry him to L.A. Hunger pangs gripped his stomach and his shoulder throbbed with pain.

So Santino had been on the case for two years. Undoubtedly, he had been at the house in the desert where Jean had made his slim escape.

He thought hard. The desert came back in a vision. He could see the house. He had flown out the back, provided a diversion; created tracks that would hopefully throw them off. The whole scenario had unfolded in minutes.

His face was close to the hot sand.

Yes, one of the guys had said the name Santino.

Santino had also brought Lilly to the airport the day LaChance had fled Tucson all those months before. Lilly had spent time with the man, but had never said much about it.

The house in the desert, the airport, the holding cell. Technically, LaChance had escaped from Santino three times.

His smile glowed orange in the dash lights. Adrenaline was seeping out of his pores; his system was slowing to base level. What a thrill. It was an amazing aphrodisiac—a very familiar emotion. He felt powerful.

His departure from the States might be only days away. His thoughts rebounded to Lilly and the kids. They were sleeping now, and the thought brought a warm rush. The taste of legitimate life had been liberating. He had discovered he could do things besides steal, and it pleased him. He wanted out as soon as possible. Despite the kick he got from skillful flight, it wasn't enough to keep him in this game.

Phoenix appeared first as a dome of light miles before he arrived. By now, he was feeling safe, but would wait to stop until he reached California. Even if his face was out in the news, very few people would see it until morning. He streaked past the city, killing time with music on the radio. He chain-smoked his way through the pack of Camels.

The California state line sign appeared in just over two hours. Relief washed over LaChance like a huge cresting wave. It wasn't necessarily any safer in California than in Arizona, but it felt like he was crossing the border into a free country. He finally stopped at a truck stop for coffee and sandwich to wake his brain and ease his grumbling stomach. He had been awake nearly twenty four hours, except for the time he was out from the hit to his head. He filled the car with gas and checked the oil. A mishap at this point would be awkward.

Now he could get to Dominic's without another stop.

He pulled next to a dumpster on the far side of the parking lot and looked around before popping the trunk and stuffing the police uniform, gun and Officer Knowles' keys into a plastic garbage bag and tying it tight. He heaved the bag into the top of the dumpster. It hit the bottom with a dark thud.

Route 177, the road to Lilly's house in the desert, came up within an hour. He was tempted to return to retrieve his photo of the family and catch some sleep, but the thought sent a chill through his body. Better to listen to instinct. Instinct would have saved him from capture in Tucson.

Dawn arrived in the California desert like a gray curtain lifting from a stage. Mile after mile drifted past the side windows in a sandy brown blur. The realization began to creep in—how lucky he had been. If one thing had gone wrong, he would still be in the cell in Tucson and the FBI would be arriving within hours.

If Officer Knowles had been more seasoned.

If the officer at the desk hadn't left his post.

If the stairs hadn't led down to an outside door.

There were so many variables that could have ended in disaster.

FBI field agents were on their way to Tucson right now. LaChance shuddered in the driver's seat. They would have interrogated him. They would've alerted French law enforcement, and Paris would have sent representatives immediately. He would have been extradited to France in shackles and locked up for a long, long time in a maximum security prison. Lilly and the kids would have been clueless. He sucked in a deep breath and stretched his neck from side to side.

Lilly.

She had been right about that part.

He had been very, very lucky.

His dark past would soon be behind him. He couldn't dare relax until he reached Dominic's house where he could catch up on sleep and plan his departure.

Dominic would have a new passport. LaChance was excited about the possibilities. He would hide out for several days and find a new disguise. Best to let the heat cool down before making an exit. Except for fatigue, he felt great.

He stretched back in the seat and allowed his mind to explore Lilly's body on the beach.

Death of the Frenchman

Chapter 25

A ribbon of tiny bubbles squeezed between the snorkel and Henry's taut upper lip. His body lay motionless on top of the water near a towering staghorn coral with tines awash in the rhythmic surf. Two huge strawberry groupers cruised near the bottom at the brink of the coral shelf.

Not yet. Not yet.

His unconscious chanted the words like a mantra. Experience with gopher hunting had taught him that potential prey would relax and even approach if he was patient and still. His 12 year old hands were beginning to shake from gripping the Hawaiian sling stretched to its full length. The groupers circled back toward deeper water, then one made the fatal mistake. It turned suddenly to look at the floating body above and Henry took his shot.

The needle-sharp point struck the grouper mid-body, bursting through to the other side. Dark blood squirted into the clear water. Henry braced himself, a death grip on the sling's rubber. The stocky fish was nearly twenty pounds, and a stronger swimmer than the boy. The grouper convulsed with a shudder and bolted for the bottom, to a hole where it would wait for death to turn its glassy eyes to jelly.

Henry allowed himself to be dragged down then kicked heavily with the fins to slow the descent and gain the surface. One last big breath had filled his lungs before the release of the spear, but the excitement of the successful strike had forced some of it out. The fish struggled for depth. Henry ignored his burning lungs and kicked again. He started to rise in the water column. Finally, with one last surge, Henry's head burst through the surface and he cleared his snorkel with the last of his air, sucking fresh oxygen back into his lungs.

"Heeeeeyyyyyyy!" Marcos cheered from his seat in the boat. "Yeah, man!"

Henry freed the mask from his face with one hand and threw it to the older boy. His teeth curled in a grin past the snorkel and he pumped hard with his legs to the side of the skiff. Marcos leaned over the side and took the sling's rubber to secure it around a cleat before offering a hand to pull Henry aboard.

"Great shot," Marcos said. "I was watching you from up here. That fish took you down some."

"I know," Henry gasped. "It was a little scary, but I got him. Come on, let's get him in."

Henry lifted the spear until the giant grouper, now dead, broke the surface. It was a great shot, mid body, just aft of the huge pectoral fin. The grouper hadn't suffered much. Marcos wedged his fingers behind the gill plate and together, they heaved the big fish into the boat. Adolescent hoots and hollers drowned out the slap of their high-fives. As if on cue, they both dove overboard to cool off.

"Man, your mother will be so happy," Marcos crowed.

"Yeah, she will be. Only the grouper is too big. We don't have any refrigeration back yet. You have to take at least half."

"Maybe we can split it up and give some to the neighbors."

Since the hurricane, Henry and Marcos were full-time fishermen. Villagers were consumed with the recovery effort, and fresh food was a blessed gift for families who had lost everything. The boys found intense purpose in their chore, the pride of providing life-giving nourishment in the midst of defeat.

Their fathers were best friends. Marcos' parents, Ramón and Leila, owned a sprawling farm two miles inland, spared from Hurricane Stephanie's full wrath due to its protected location. Ramón was several generations deep in the island's culture, a respected member of the community. He knew men like Jean LaChance. They were trustworthy, loyal to the end, and so the boys had become natural allies.

Marcos was the first friend Henry could remember. Life without a father had yoked Henry to his younger siblings; stolen his childhood. He was shy and guarded by nature, disinclined to organized sports or games. Industry was more his niche, and he was a born hunter; patient, observant, quiet. Killing was simply part of the job—not that he enjoyed it. Occasionally, he recalled his first gopher—before Jean had come into their lives.

He had been alone above the gopher town behind the house in the California desert. The small gun kicked, the gopher in his sights flipped over and lay still. Henry's head jerked up, doubtful he had hit the animal. He had stood and walked over to the ground squirrel. The blond body looked much smaller in death than it had in life, minus the head. Hurtful tears pushed their way out of his eyes, and he glanced around to make certain no one had borne witness to the gruesome murder. Grief and guilt poured through his veins, and he had left the dead animal where it lay and returned to the house. His secret weighed on him until he found his mother crying late at night on the front porch.

"Mom?"

Lilly had hurriedly brushed the tears away and pretended to be fixing her hair.

"What honey?"

"Are you okay? Are you crying?"

The six little words started an avalanche of tears and fears. Dewey had been absent for weeks. Food was sparse. The nearest store was miles away and might as well have been in outer space. Meals consisted of potatoes or pasta with any kind of flavor or spice she could invent from the nothing they had. They had no car, not much money, and little hope of breaking free from the frightening isolation that crushed her with worry for her children. Henry had returned to the gopher town the next day and came home with a cloth bag full of the little creatures. That day, he hadn't cried.

Lilly was horrified at the sight of the headless creatures that looked like abbreviated furry-tailed rats. But she knew something about wildlife, knew these particular rodents were abundant and ate grass, so they were most likely edible. Skinning and gutting their tiny bodies was a chore, but once the fur was gone and the legs chopped at the knees, they resembled something you might see in a foreign butcher shop. She fried one carcass and tested it, surprised at the sweet taste of the meat. From that day on, the fear of feeding her children was gone. Henry had become their provider.

The move from their house in the desert to Tucson had ended Henry's hunting responsibilities, which stole his thoughts through endless classroom days of math and English studies that were tedium for his restless mind. He drudged through the exercises, staring at the clock hands as they crept in a steady circle until the last bell released him from scholastic prison. At last, May arrived and with it, a post card from Jean that beckoned the family to the island.

Henry was free once again. Though his mother begged him, forced him to sit and study in the home school classroom of the veranda, she eventually admitted defeat. Henry would never be a willing student, not of books and numbers. While Amos and Sherri pored over their lessons at the table with Lilly, Henry crossed the threshold to the working world by his eleventh birthday, and in doing so, discovered the addiction of the clear deep water embracing the island.

Marco's father, Ramón had eight children, five boys and three girls in a convenient order that provided working staff for the farm and child care for the younger ones. Marcos had begun his fishing career with his father as a toddler, and by age ten, was operating the boat solo, freeing his father to run the farm. But he was social by nature, and the isolation drove him crazy. Henry's arrival provided not only a partner, but an adept hunter.

The two years together cemented the friendship. They cruised into every little inlet they could find—exploring outcroppings of rocks and shelves of coral that housed great schools of fish; grouper, jack, grunts and snapper, a virtual underwater supermarket at their disposal.

Marcos preferred fishing above the water with a weight and line, but the first time Henry held a spear in his hands, it felt much like his long-gone rifle. He was a strong swimmer, even without the bulky fins Jean had purchased for him. While Marcos sat with his hand line above, Henry pursued his prey below. They never returned home empty-handed.

Before the hurricane, their catch was sold to the two restaurants in the village or to cruisers, bringing good money for two boys fifteen and twelve. Though Lilly worried about him out on the ocean, she was proud. Jean began to treat him like a man. He stopped tousling Henry's wild hair and used adult language, even discussing the business of the guest house like an equal partner. Henry submitted a percentage of his income to Jean on a weekly basis, aware his parents didn't need his money. The contribution fed his grownup persona. Forced into adulthood at eight years old, he wore responsibility like an old boot. Jean took the cash with casual thanks, and stashed it in a separate fund for supplies Henry required. A new boat sporting a 4-stroke outboard would make a long-deserved reward.

The boys hoisted the skiff's anchor and raced into the late day sun along the sandy shore to the village. The sturdy grouper required all four hands to reach the surface of the cleaning board on the village dock. Marcos wielded the fillet knife with the expertise of a Japanese chef, and soon the fat skeins of white meat lay shiny and clean alongside the massive head. Marcos' neighbor, an old woman named Señora Rodrigo with a reputation for delectable fish-head soup would be the lucky recipient.

They high-fived and parted with "Hasta mañanas." Marcos jumped onto his bike and Henry shouldered his share of the grouper and headed along the waterfront. Village women hailed him along his walk, spying the plump bag slung on his shoulder. Every one of them had received a gift fish from Henry. They loved the quiet little white boy, and often complimented his remarkable dreadlocks.

Henry saw the hair style as a sign he belonged here. Caucasian dreadlocks were practically non-existent. On occasion, he had seen surfers from Europe or America around the village, many of them forcing their normally sleek hair into a dread-like coif resembling a mangled dirty mop. Henry's natural ringlets had made the hairdo easier to achieve. He kept his hair clean, and twisted the strands as he was instructed by Black Walter down at the docks. After several months of dedicated twisting, a haircut was no longer necessary, he told his mother.

Amos sat outside the tent entertaining Evie. The child squealed at Henry's arrival.

"Hey," Henry offered.

"Hey," Amos returned. "Wow, nice catch. Can I see?"

Henry kissed the top of Evie's head and playfully whacked his brother's arm before opening the bag. Amos slapped him back on the shoulder and both boys grinned. They loved each other, and missed their time together. The tedium of babysitting left Amos without real conversation. He watched with envy as Henry left in the mornings. He impatiently awaited his freedom from domesticity.

"Mom's gonna cry," he said, with a small glint in his eye. The catch was admirable. His face said so.

"Maybe," Henry chuckled.

"That's too much for one meal," said Amos. "I wonder if Tia Maria needs food."

The brothers had never tasted the sweet coffee liqueur, were not even sure what it was, but since newcomers always chuckled at the name of the crusty old woman, they pretended to get the joke.

"That's a good idea. Wanna go with me?"

Amos' brows jumped. Tia Maria's house was two miles down the road in the direction of the airstrip. He hadn't been that far from home since before the hurricane.

"What about Evie?"

"I'm sure Mom will take her. Come on."

Amos was right. Lilly took one look in Henry's bag and started to cry. The boys exchanged a grin behind their mother's back.

"It's too much," she sniffed.

"I know. Marcos took the other half and the head for Señora Rodrigo. I thought maybe me and Amos could take a piece to Tia Maria."

"Amos and I."

"Okay."

"Okay what?"

"I thought maybe me and Amos and I could take a piece to Tia Maria."

Amos fell over with laughter. Lilly slapped Henry's arm lightly and shot Amos a stern smile. She hated improper grammar and corrected Henry's verbal butchery every time he slipped, though Jean had warned her months ago:

"He'll only keep it up, you know. Don't ride him. He'll turn it around eventually."

"And this advice comes from all of your child-rearing experience, does it?" she asked.

Jean smiled and shrugged his shoulders.

"Whatever you want, my love," he said. "I just think there's a possibility that he does it on purpose—to get to you."

"It doesn't 'get to me,' I just want him to speak proper English."

"He does speak proper English, and his Spanish is better than any of us. Ramón says he sounds like a local."

"All that time with Marcos."

"If it makes you feel any better, when Marcos speaks English he says 'me and Henry' too," Jean said, and Lilly was forced to laugh. So proud.

The memory stopped Lilly for a second.

God, she missed him. Where was he? When was he coming home?

Lilly lifted the fillet onto the cutting board and admired the whiteness of the meat. She cut off a generous piece for the boys to deliver and returned it to the bag.

"We'll see you in an hour," she said, and blew kisses at both boys. "Oh, and Henry, thank you, honey. Good job, really."

The boy grinned and touched his mother's shoulder.

"You're welcome, ma'am," he said in a deep cowboy drawl.

As soon as the tent flap had fallen back down, a bellow exploded from Evie. Amos jerked to a stop.

"Come on, let her cry," Henry said. "If you don't, she'll get to be a cry baby. She'll get really demanding, and then when she gets older, we'll be in big trouble."

Amos' brow crinkled.

"How do you know?" he asked defensively. He had taken care of Evie since her birth, and considered himself a pro.

Henry looked between his dreads.

"Remember when Dad left?" His tone meant their biological knew which dad Henry meant.

"Nah, I don't really remember him at all. Maybe a little. He was kinda muscly, wasn't he?"

"Yeah, I guess he played football in high school."

"Really?"

Lilly never discussed the kids' father, as if they had, indeed, been delivered by storks, or some miraculous virgin birth.

"Well, I remember him pretty good. He wasn't much of a dad."

"Did he hit you?"

Henry's face shot up to look at his brother. It was strange question. It was also true, a couple of times.

"Why, do you remember that?"

"I remember fights. They were really loud."

"Yeah, I remember fights, too." Henry had popped out of his mother a natural guardian. He had put himself in the line of fire as far back as his short memory would go.

"Did he hurt Mom?"

"Sometimes I think he tried to. He used to drink a lot. I think he might've been mad that he had kids."

"I don't remember what his voice sounded like."

"Lucky bastard." The boys laughed at the forbidden word. "Mostly it was either yelling or slurring."

"Wow."

They walked along in silence for a stretch. Bananaquits flitted and chirped through the tangled brush on the side of the road, the only sound in the late, still afternoon.

"Anyway, why did you bring him up?" Amos asked finally.

"Oh, because Sherri was three, a lot older than Evie is now, but I was in charge of her, both of you guys. She got really whiny after Dad left and Mom taught me to ignore her when it was right. She said that Sherri would grow up to be a cry baby."

"Sometimes she is a cry baby."

"See?"

They laughed.

They climbed the narrow road to the top of the first rise. The sandy surface became patchy broken pavement laid more than twenty years before. A steady rhythm of two pairs of slapping feet bounced against the short garden walls, their tough soles immune to the rough surface. Shoes were so distant a memory, they would be a hazard on the uneven road.

"When do you think Jean's coming back?" Amos asked.

Sherri had started calling Jean "Daddy" almost immediately when they arrived on the island, even before the wedding made the title legitimate. Amos took a little longer, but it gradually worked its way into his vocabulary. Henry observed this, but held off until just recently. That word from Henry's mouth put a shocked smile on LaChance's face. But the boys usually called him "Jean" when they spoke to each other.

"I don't know," Henry said softly. It had been two weeks. The fear crept deeper with every passing day, but he pushed it aside for his family, especially his mother.

"I know he knows what he's doing," Henry added. "He'll be okay," he said, almost believing his own words.

"Yeah," Amos said. "It's been a long time, though, hasn't it?"

"About two weeks." Henry knew exactly how long. Two weeks and one day.

"Mom's really worried."

"I know."

"He went back to get the money, didn't he?"

"Yeah, I think so."

"Hope it's safe."

"Me too."

Amos threw his arm up to Henry's near shoulder. He had a caretaker's spirit. Henry struggled with gestures and words of affection that were second nature to his little brother. The move narrowed the gap between them. Henry put his arm over the top of Amos'.

"Do you know what Dad did before?" asked Amos. This time, the word meant Jean.

"I guess he was a thief."

"Oh."

"That doesn't make him a bad guy."

"I know, I just think about it sometimes. Does Mom tell you stuff about him?"

"Not stuff like that." Henry paused for a while. "I guess he did that for a long time."

Amos wiped his face with the back of his hand.

"Do you think it's wrong? I mean, he stole stuff, right? Money and maybe other things."

"Yeah," Henry said.

Henry worshipped Jean. Usually he could keep these thoughts at bay, but the conflict about right and wrong touched a nerve.

"Wow," Amos said. His soft voice was free of judgment; in fact, the tone was admiration. "I bet he's really good, like, picking locks and stuff."

"Don't talk about it that way. It's not a TV show."

"I'm not. I'm just saying; he's so smart and good at everything. You saw him shoot, right?"

"Yeah, he's a really good shot."

"Yeah."

"Yeah."

"Wonder if he ever shot anybody." The boys looked up at each other.

"I asked him that when we were in Tucson," Henry said.

"What did he say?"

"He didn't answer."

"Probably not, then," Amos said.

"Yeah, probably not."

They were about half way to Tia Maria's house. The sun sagged toward the horizon, dropping long cool shadows across the road. The boys walked in and out, in and out of the sun beams. Henry scooped up a rock and flung it off the side of the road.

"Evie's really talking a lot now," Henry said.

"Yeah, sometimes she talks constantly."

"At least you know what she's saying."

Amos cracked up.

"I guess. Don't you understand her?"

"Not really. Sometimes it sounds like a foreign language. Do you like taking care of her?"

"It's okay. Sometimes it's boring. She's fun though. I don't know."

"If you don't want to do it, you should tell Mom."

"Yeah. No, it's not that I don't want to do it. You do a lot of stuff, and I guess I never did. Sherri's too little."

"Sherri's too little now, but she'll be old enough pretty soon."

"Yeah."

Henry clapped his hand on Amos' back. The younger boy smiled. Henry was his idol.

"I think you're doing a great job."

"Thanks," Amos said softly.

Suddenly, their conversation was over. They walked in silence the rest of the way. Tia Maria was giddy and gruff and bear-hugged the boys with sinewy arms. The round trip took over an hour. It was nearly dark when they got back to the tent.

Henry put an arm on Amos' shoulder just outside the tent flap. Their eyes met.

"Dad's gonna be okay," Henry said. "Really. He's coming home soon."

"Yeah, I know," Amos answered, but they stood looking at each other for some time, trying to convince themselves it was true.

Chapter 26

Santino's cell phone rang him awake at three in the morning. He knew before he answered it that the caller would have bad news, and that the news would be about Jean LaChance. He had considered sleeping at the station just to make sure the Frenchman stayed in his cell.

Santino had read LaChance's dossier. It was impressive. Impossible heists had been executed by him or simply attributed to him without proper evidence, because there wasn't another suspect capable of the intricate logistics. Many of Paris' tricky unsolved cases had been pinned on LaChance. French law enforcement could never keep up with him, and now the Tucson police had joined that thwarted club.

Santino raced to the police station within ten minutes of the call. Disgust forced bile into his throat. What had happened? Something stupid, he guessed. He had seen the cell. It was inescapable within that time frame. Some anxious cop had pulled a bonehead move, and now LaChance was on the loose. Santino knew they'd never catch him now. He was far too smart, too capable. He knew they had his face, his name. He'd disappear, and the law would never again hear anything from the notorious Frenchman.

The police station was a flurry of activity, with numerous cruisers in chaotic formation outside, all the lights flashing. Santino had to produce identification to gain entry. Uniforms spread wall-to-wall. Hectic conversation filled the front desk area. Roadblocks were being organized and officers deployed to the streets in the immediate area to search for the escapee.

Santino shook his head. LaChance was probably halfway to nowhere by this time. He asked a couple of questions and was directed to Captain Harrison. The Captain had been his Tucson contact two years before. Typically, a private investigator would not be allowed inside police operations, but Harrison respected

Santino's perseverance on the case and his former detective title. He invited Santino to join them in a small interrogation room behind the desk.

Officer Knowles sat in a chair on one side of the table massaging his throat. He was dressed in an oversized orange jumpsuit. Jesus, thought Santino. Fucking LaChance even got his clothes. He nodded at the Captain and dropped down on a chair opposite the rookie.

"So what the hell happened?" Santino asked. His face was tight with anger.

"I don't know, sir. I took him a cup of water . . ."

"And he disabled you through the bars, huh?" Santino finished his sentence. "Jesus Christ! Weren't you listening in class?" He didn't mind condescending to the kid. It had been absolutely stupid.

"Yes, sir, I was listening, it's just that he was in pain, and I didn't think . . ."

"Bingo! You got that right, Knowles. You didn't think. Christ, guys like LaChance don't feel pain. Did you bother to look at his record? He's one of the most capable crooks in fucking history! They oughta pull your badge."

"LaChance took care of that for him," the Captain answered from the door.

"You lost your fucking badge, too?" Santino snapped. "You're a moron. Christ! The Feds will be here in a couple of hours. We had the guy, something the French police haven't been able to do in fucking thirty years! Why did you hand him a cup of water? He wasn't going to dehydrate overnight. I supposed he got your gun, too!"

Knowles didn't answer this one. He was hanging his head and wishing the shame game was over.

"I know, I know. It was stupid."

"Fucking right, it was stupid. What a disgrace. Now we have to face those Feds in the morning. They love shit like this. Local cops foiled by internationally famous thief in the wee hours—Tucson, Arizona. Get used to hearing it, kid. It'll be all over the news."

Santino was done talking to the officer. He knew he wouldn't learn anything new, and he was starting to lose his temper. He left the room with the Captain and stepped back into the chaos of the station.

"I'm sorry Harrison. I didn't mean to lean on him so hard, but Jesus."

"That's all right. He should hear it again and again so he remembers it next time."

"Listen, I know you guys have to sweep the neighborhood and set up roadblocks and everything, but I'll tell you what—LaChance is gone. He's way too savvy to get caught now that he knows we're onto him. The surprise for him ended at the bank. What the fuck happened, Captain?"

The Captain shook his head.

"I'm not sure. I guess the kid wanted a look at LaChance, so he went inside and asked him if he was hungry, then LaChance asked for some water. When he handed LaChance the cup, it was all over for Knowles. He's damn lucky to be alive, if you ask me."

"I'm sure he's capable, but LaChance isn't a killer. He wouldn't want the FBI after him for killing a cop. I guess there's never been one death attributed to him."

"Interesting. LaChance probably has all the moves. He took out four cops at the bank until they beaned him. He choked Knowles, took his uniform and keys and then locked him in the cell. Then he stood inside the door until the officer at the desk turned his head for a split second, and he was out and down the stairs, where he took out another cop and lifted his keys. They didn't know anything until they heard the alarm for the outside door. That's never happened here before."

"You've never had anybody like LaChance in here before, either."

"You're right about that," the Captain said.

"I know it's too early, but expect a report of a stolen vehicle in this immediate area by morning, and he won't drive that car very far. Has anyone been sent to the bank? LaChance might have picked up his vehicle there. He didn't have anything on him but the identification for the safe-deposit box. No keys, no gun, no tools, nothing. He might have left them in a car, but I'll bet the stolen vehicle is there somewhere close to the bank."

"Richards! We got somebody over at the bank where they got the French guy, don't we? We're looking for a stolen vehicle, but it probably won't be reported for a couple of hours."

"Any idea where we should be looking for LaChance?" the Captain asked Santino.

"Sorry. Not a clue. The guy is a real ghost, I'll tell you that. He could've gone in any direction. We don't have any records of LaChance or David Smith clearing customs or immigration in the last two weeks. He probably has a whole catalog of aliases. He's got good connections somewhere, no doubt. If I had to guess, I would say he came in through LAX. When he left France four years ago, he went straight to L.A., from what we can figure. He had to have a reason to go there. There was no news on him until he and Dewey Jensen robbed Richard Prescott's house in October, two years back. The only reason we had anything was because Jensen's prints were everywhere, and they were the only ones at Prescott's house. He was a small-timer with a whole string of clumsy arrests, mostly misdemeanors. According to old man Prescott, there was a hooker who probably discovered Prescott's little treasure chest by accident and told Jensen. Jensen needed LaChance to access the house, which was alarmed, of course. We caught up with Jensen a couple weeks later, dead as a mackerel out behind his house in the desert not far from Joshua Tree, California. LaChance was there, too. At least his prints were all over the house. Jensen was killed with a .22, of all things. We don't know LaChance did it, but I'll lay odds he doesn't carry a .22. There was a woman, Jensen's former girlfriend Lilly Parsons and her three kids. I don't know, could've been one of the kids who killed Jensen. We never found the rifle. Get this—there were skinned gophers in the freezer. I think they were living on gophers."

"Wow," said the Captain. "Where is this Lilly Parsons?"

"We finally found her in Tucson, with the kids. They weren't trying to hide. They denied everything, even the kids, but we got LaChance's prints, well, matching prints anyway all over the house. We took her to the airport—they were planning to leave that day. Anyway, somehow she warned him. We never saw him. He flew out right from under our noses. That was my fuck up. We didn't have an ID on the guy at the time, so we didn't know who we were looking for. We had nothing on her, so the case was dead. Then the next May, Lilly and kids disappear, off the face of the planet. She didn't even contact the kids' school, or her mother, although I paid Mom a visit in June, and she seemed to have come into some money. Big surprise, huh? We never found any of the money—close to one million in cash. So in two years, not a word from any of them, until David Smith resurfaced at the banks yesterday. We almost didn't get him then. Another five minutes, and he would've been gone. He's good at that."

"How did you get all this information on LaChance?"

"It bugged the shit out of me, him slipping away any time we got close. The department was leaning on me pretty hard, so I retired, but I couldn't let it go. I figured the key was the prints we couldn't identify, so I ran them through a friend who has better connections than I do. That took a while, as you can probably guess. That's how we got his original I.D. He's a chameleon. I really gotta hand it to the guy. He's a piece of work. I talked to him last night. I mean, I talked. The only thing he asked was the time. That's the only thing he said. He's like ice. To tell you the truth, I was glad the bars were there. He's one intimidating motherfucker."

The Captain drew in a deep breath and let it out slowly.

"Well, I guess we should get ready for the Feds. This is gonna stink."

Death of the Frenchman

"Got that right. I'll bet Knowles wants to go home."
The Captain laughed.
"Poor kid. He just got too impressed."
"Can't blame him. I'm impressed, too."

Chapter 27

Dominic answered the phone on the first ring.

"Dominic. Jean."

"Man, you okay? You're all over the news."

"Yes, I'm fine. I'm just checking that it's safe to go there. I'm pretty hot right now."

"Yeah, come on. Park in the back."

Jean hung up and went straight to Dominic's house. He was completely spent. Horrible spasms of pain shot through his head and into his shoulder. Dominic sent him into the shower and from there, LaChance collapsed onto the bed and slept all day. When he woke up, it was already dark.

They sat on the deck sipping Scotch and smoking. Dominic's girlfriend went out for pizza. LaChance relayed the events of the last couple of days, and his friend sat quietly listening.

"Wow, man, huh?" Dominic said. "You lucky bastard. That could've gone bad, any of it."

"I know. I was really lucky. It was pretty close. Another couple of hours, and the Feds would have me. You'd have never seen me again."

"Jesus," Dominic said. "Good thing you know what you're doing."

"That helps, of course," LaChance said. "But I was lucky. I shouldn't have had that chance with the cop."

Dominic reached for the bottle and poured Jean another glass of Scotch.

"Now they know your face. David Smith and Jean LaChance are done, aren't they? What do you want to do?"

"Rest, for a couple of days. Let the heat cool down. I'll need that passport. Let's do a great disguise, maybe make me really old, dark, with glasses, curly hair, big nose, the works. All I have to do is get out. I think if I wait at least a week, they'll be a bit more relaxed, but it might be a good idea to fly from somewhere besides L.A. I'm thinking maybe drive into Mexico and fly from there. Either way I just want to sit still for a while and recover."

"How are you feeling?"

"A little rough. My shoulder of course, then the cops in the bank whacked me pretty good." He dropped his head and showed Dominic the wound. "That still hurts. I should probably get stitches. Maybe you could help with that. I'm pretty beat up."

He took a drink of the Scotch and looked at his friend.

"I'm getting too old for this," Jean laughed.

Dominic chuckled.

"Well, you're done, aren't you?"

"I hope so," Jean said. "Running a hotel is easier on my nerves."

Dominic's girlfriend, Maria, came in with two large pizzas, set them down on the table and kissed her boyfriend. She was a beautiful girl, and new to LaChance. She disappeared into the house for paper towels and silverware.

"She's a beautiful woman," Jean said.

"Yeah, thanks man. She's a great lady."

"It's wonderful, isn't it? Being with a lady you love."

"Never thought I'd hear you say that," Dominic said, taking the utensils from Maria. "Maria is a nurse. Maybe she could look at your head."

Jean lifted his drink and tipped it in her direction.

"Thank you, that would be lovely."

"How is Lilly, by the way?"

"I have no idea. I would think the phones are still down. She's fine, I'm sure. The kids are great. They help all the time. A friend is looking in on them every day. I wish I could talk to her, though."

He directed his next comment to Maria.

"You women," he said. "You're amazing. You have a way of making everything better. I feel like my life started the day I met Lilly."

"That's because we're complete people. You guys are a little undercooked."

The men laughed.

"Well, I'm glad you're here, Jean. Just take it easy for a couple of days," Dominic said. "I'll start tomorrow on finalizing your passport, photos and all that. We'll figure out something failsafe for you. It'll be great to have you around for a while."

Jean reached for a piece of pizza and smiled. Thank God for Dominic. He would've been dead on the street.

Chapter 28

Agents arrived from the Phoenix FBI field office by 9:00 a.m. the morning of LaChance's escape. Just as Santino suspected, they wore subtle smug expressions as they listened to the string of events that resulted in the escape of the famous thief. Officer Knowles was a pitiful sight in a borrowed, ill-fitting uniform. After the initial details of Knowles' stupidity, the agents largely ignored him, saving their interrogation for Captain Brower, who was guilty by accountability.

Everyone crowded into one large conference room to watch an FBI presentation of Jean LaChance's dossier on a screen pulled from the ceiling. Within minutes, the room was stifling from the heat of the projector accentuated by the odor of the sweaty men. Very few photos of LaChance were produced, but his record, largely speculation, filled each frame—dates, victims, locations worldwide where the Frenchman had left his mark. Priceless art, jewelry, minerals, technological prototypes, specialty items, gold bullion, and family heirlooms, not to mention millions in cash and bonds, had all disappeared into LaChance's hands.

The Tucson cops sat motionless, staring numbly at the screen. With every minute, Knowles' mistake became a misstep worthy of empathy. The Frenchman was a genius, a true artist of the underworld. They had had the Rembrandt of thieves locked up within their very own station, if for a few hours.

Santino watched the presentation with mixed emotions, angry that LaChance was loose; bursting with pride that he himself had provided the catalyst for the man's capture. The FBI was serious about LaChance. Agents had been dispatched throughout cities within a thousand mile radius. The FBI was the best of the best. If anyone could catch the Frenchman, they could. But Santino doubted it would happen any time soon.

The presentation finished before noon, and the agents packed their files, excused themselves, and left as quickly as they had arrived. They were done with the Tucson Police Department. Santino shook a few hands and exchanged business cards. He found himself with little else to do but go home.

The early wakeup call had left him without a shower or a shave, so he returned to the hotel and ended up face down on the bed, fully clothed. He slept until 2:00 a.m.

The roar of a motorcycle outside his window opened his eyes, and he was unable to fall asleep again, so he got up, showered and shaved, dressed in clean clothes and checked out of the hotel. He would be back in L.A. well before the evening rush hour.

The lonely highway disappearing into blackness allowed him some welcomed thinking time. He reached the California state line just as dawn was waking the desert. It was a clear, cloudless October day with not a whisper of wind to stir the sand. He glanced down at the twenty-something year old face of his adversary riding shotgun beside him.

"Where are you now, my friend?" he asked out loud. It seemed that he could look into the man in the photo. He envied LaChance's mind; his skill. The menacing vision of LaChance behind bars came back in a rush. How many men had that power? None he had ever met. The Frenchman had become an obsession, a quarry worthy of the chase. He had found him once. Maybe he could do it again.

The miles ticked by as Santino fed his fantasy of pursuit and capture. Up ahead, he saw signs for an intersection and realized that he was approaching Route 177, the highway where Lilly had lived with the kids, the house where Dewey Jensen's life had ended, the location of Santino's first encounter with the famous French thief. He turned north on the highway. With LaChance on the run, there was plenty of time and nowhere to go. He might as well return to the original scene of a crime that had haunted him for two years.

Mile marker 256 was as he recalled; non-descript—a small dirt track leading off the pavement that was easily missed from a passing car. He stopped just off the highway and got out to examine the road. Recent tire tracks turned from the south onto the dirt track. There were two sets, likely coming and going. What did that mean? Maybe someone was living in the isolated house. The sight of the tracks made the hair on his neck stand to attention.

He drove the punishing mile slow enough to prevent damage to the under carriage of his car. The tire tracks led him like a beacon straight to the front porch steps. Someone had driven in, then backed out and turned around. Whoever it was had been there in the past few days. Could it have been LaChance? Why would he return here? Was there something he needed from the house?

Santino ascended the front porch steps and entered the house. Everything looked just as they had left it. A thick layer of yellow dust coated every surface in the kitchen. He opened the refrigerator and slammed it closed immediately. The food inside had long since turned into an amorphous pile of goo that emitted a horrendous odor. He checked the backyard and then climbed the stairs. The rooms reflected the cops' search for Richard Prescott's money. The bureaus were mostly empty and only a few articles of clothing hung in the closets. It looked like no one had been there for two years.

Santino checked Lilly's room last. Instantly, he noticed the mattress, which lay perfectly straight on the low bed frame, the solo orderly item in the room. Clothes and shoes were scattered chaotically on the floor. One single folded article of clothing lay on the bureau with a photo on top. He walked slowly over to the bureau, his heart beat increasing in tempo. Though it had been two years since Santino had seen them, he instantly recognized Lilly and the kids. Santino flipped the photo over. There was nothing written on the back. Unlike every other surface in the house, the photo was clean. It had been placed there recently. LaChance had been here. He sat down on the bed and took out his glasses.

The small snapshot was current. Not only were the three kids visibly older, but Lilly was holding a baby about a year old on her hip. A check for prints was unnecessary. Santino knew LaChance's were on it. He looked closer at the picture.

The little family was standing on a beach. The kids were laughing, and Lilly was frozen in the act of blowing a kiss toward the photographer with her free hand. LaChance had taken this photo. Though nothing in the picture identified the location, Santino could see something in the background that might help. It was a boat.

He grabbed the blouse, raced down the stairs and out the front door. He rummaged through the glove box for a magnifying glass. The faces of the family bounced out from the photo under the glass, and Santino focused it on the boat anchored out behind the family in the water. It was a dark blue sailboat with two masts. A Jolly Roger hung from a flag halyard. Though he could not see a name on the hull, the boat looked unique, identifiable. The photo couldn't be too old, possibly several months. The boat might still be in that general vicinity.

He could not imagine why LaChance would have left the photo behind, except for the diversion it might have caused from the business at the banks. It probably never occurred to the Frenchman that anyone would return to the house, and he would never throw it away. The blouse was surely Lilly's. The ritualistic placement of the photo was tender, meaningful.

Santino lifted the blouse to his face and inhaled deeply. Sure enough, it had the scent of a woman. He smiled.

LaChance was in love. Nothing else would explain the ceremonial position of the family photo atop Lilly's blouse. He had returned to the scene where he had fallen in love. Santino had finally found it. The Frenchman's weakness was, of course, a woman.

Chapter 29

The following several days were nirvana. Apart from working up a new disguise with the aid of Dominic's contact, LaChance had very little to do. Exposure was his only concern. His face was plastered all over the news, compliments of The FBI. He stayed inside Dominic's house, wishing he still had the photo of Lilly and the kids.

The disguise that he and Dominic created was of a much older man, perhaps in his 70s or 80s, with a long gray beard, bulbous nose, numerous age spots, and large, blurry glasses. He walked with the aid of a cane. LaChance practiced a convincing limp and gravelly voice with the coach, a multi-talented Hollywood make-up artist named Billy. After a couple of hours, the talented LaChance could easily pass for an old man. All he had to do was get out of the country. Once he landed in Lima, he could use any identity for safe travel to Venezuela and on to the island.

LaChance felt relatively safe, but mulled over the wisdom of a departure from LAX. The passport and other supporting paperwork were in place. He and Dominic sat and talked late into the night on his third day in L.A.

"What do you think about flying out from LAX?" Jean asked.

"Don't know. Could be bad. Could be nothing. The disguise is great. I would never know it was you. Once you get to South America, you're relatively safe. On the other hand, I'm not certain this news hasn't reached Lima, so just be sure to not get too full of yourself."

The men laughed. The trust they shared was air tight. Dominic owed LaChance his life, and both men were aware of the weight of that debt. Dominic would help where he could, but he also had to fly low. None of his income was legitimate. Addresses he had supplied LaChance for use in the States were for vacant lots or abandoned buildings. He had served Jean well, paying back the debt for his life in spectacular fashion. He was the best friend the friendless LaChance could imagine.

"How will Lilly know when you are coming home?" Dominic asked.

"She won't. Not until I arrive, although the way the news travels there, I wouldn't be surprised if she would know the minute the wheels touch the airstrip. I tried to phone today, but the phones are still down. I'm not surprised. It's only been several weeks. It might take months. It won't matter. I know we're safe there, at least for now."

They discussed the mailing of the cash and communications between L.A. and the distant Caribbean island. The Italian man finally leaned back in his seat and put his hands behind his head.

"Jean," he asked. "Why did you do this? You have to have plenty of money. It doesn't make sense that you jeopardized everything just to retrieve that amount of cash."

Only a friend would dare ask this question. It was against Dominic's nature to ask, but he had a point. Over the years, LaChance had amassed a healthy sum, more than enough to retire, even with Lilly and the kids. Much of the money was in investments and secure bank accounts. LaChance was good with money, and his lifestyle had never required much. His needs had been simple; rented flats, used cars. He had secured a vision of the future, free from the underground existence of a criminal; a legitimate living, something simpler, less stressful.

Lilly had derailed his tight-rope lifestyle. He saw the trust, the gratitude and happiness she spread, from a life with very little. She had had nothing, but shared everything. It was humbling. Impressive. He had been selfish and self-concerned. Nothing but success in his craft mattered. The most remarkable aspect of Lilly was that even if she didn't agree with his chosen lifestyle, she withheld judgment and supported him without demand.

Dominic was right. It didn't make sense. LaChance had told Lilly that they needed the cash, and of course, she had believed him. With the electricity down on the island, their finances were a little tight, but as soon as it was functioning, money was available at the push of a button.

"You don't miss much," LaChance said.

"It's my job to not miss."

"You're right, I didn't need the cash. We would have done alright without the Tucson money. But, if Dewey Jensen hadn't given me directions to Lilly's house, my life would be what it was before, which, looking back wasn't much. At first, I thought I was following Lilly and the kids for the money. It was never about the money. I had to see her again. I had to be with her and the kids, if I could, if they would have me. It was the biggest change of my life."

He paused and took a drink of his beer.

"Something... something about the fact that I wouldn't know Lilly if we hadn't pulled that job—I needed to recover that. I also had to do it for me, to return to my former life just to make sure. I figured the law wouldn't go that far for someone with no identity. I know now, it was stupid. I took a chance. Now they know who I am. I can't ever come back here once I get out."

He leaned forward toward his friend. His eyes were like lasers. He sat for some seconds.

"I had to get it, you know? It was my ego driving me, but I had to beat them. I was lucky, Dominic. I should have stayed locked up for a long, long time. I'm done. It's over."

Their eyes locked for several seconds. The men had an unspoken pact from long ago.

"Let me know if you need anything, anything in the future. You know I'm always here for you, man."

"Thank you," the Frenchman said, tipping his glass.

Vulnerability. Mortality. Loyalty. All emotions that suddenly had power over LaChance's options. He was done simply because he no longer had a choice.

****

Pierre LaPorte's rental car was returned four days later by Dominic without any questions from the rental company. The following morning, Tom Roberts climbed stiffly out of a taxi at LAX. He braced his cane against the pavement and dug through his pockets for the fare. His gait was so affected, one of the airport attendants stopped to ask if he could assist. Mr. Roberts allowed the man to open the door but refused a lift on the golf cart, claiming the exercise was good for his heart.

He hobbled slowly to the airline desk, accepted his boarding pass with a warm smile and headed for security. As Mr. Roberts neared the security checkpoint, he spied a panting Belgian Shepherd guarding the entrance to the feeder line. A tall burly officer wearing an impeccable uniform held the leash. Mr. Roberts stopped and eyed the dog with suspicion.

"Excuse me," he motioned to the officer.

"Yes?"

"I'm deathly afraid of dogs. During my childhood, the Germans always used dogs during the war, and I'm terrified of those breeds. Please, please understand. Please," he pleaded. He sniffed slightly and dabbed his nose with a trembling handkerchief.

"I'm sorry sir. He won't hurt you. Just walk past him and try to ignore him."

The dog sat alert, ears perked. He pointed his muzzle at Mr. Roberts.

"I'm sorry, please, officer please; I can't pass this dog. He knows I am afraid of him. He might grab me."

"Sir, this dog is specially trained to detect drugs. If you are not carrying drugs, he won't approach you. I will assist you in getting past him if you like, but we require everyone to pass the dog when they enter security."

Bingo. Other passengers were filing past Mr. Roberts to join the queue leading to the luggage scanner. The old man took several steps, using his cane for balance. His face was lined with distress, and a small high wail escaped his throat as he passed close enough to the shepherd for the dog to reach out and touch his jacket. When he was well past the dog, he looked back at the officer with tears in his eyes.

"I'm so sorry," he said.

"That's just fine, sir. Have a good flight."

He placed his cane lengthwise on the conveyor, and held the upright of the scanner to steady himself. The security officer waited with a smile and an outstretched hand for the elderly gentleman. Mr. Roberts shuffled down the long American Airlines concourse, leaning heavily on the cane. Passengers dressed in business attire zoomed by dragging wheeled suitcases and speaking into cell phones.

There were cops everywhere. They stood alone or in pairs along the concourse, performing close visual checks of the travelers. Several looked closely at Mr. Roberts, who smiled and gave a small nod. He stopped directly in front of two officers, pulled off his glasses and cleaned them slowly with the corner of his handkerchief, his cane hanging from his forearm.

"It's good to see the presence of police officers here at the airport," he said quietly as he placed his glasses back on his face and turned to the policemen.

"Yes sir," one of the men said.

"It feels safer to fly. Flying is stressful enough by itself."

"Don't you worry, sir. We've got our eyes open."

"That's great news," the old man said. "Thank you officers."

He resumed his unhurried course, arriving at the gate forty minutes prior to departure. He sat down with effort next to a man focused on a ream of papers.

Death of the Frenchman

He placed his hands carefully on the handle of his cane and contemplated life around him. He smiled at a baby sitting on his mother's lap across the aisle, and the child's face broke into a huge grin. They played peek-a-boo for fifteen minutes.

The sudden announcement startled him. It was a departure for Lima, Peru. Mr. Roberts rose with a groan and limped to the gate. A smiley attendant took his boarding pass and thanked him for flying American Airlines. The old man walked slowly into the jet way, pausing to let a few others board in front of him and took the seat indicated on his boarding pass.

Jean LaChance, a.k.a Thomas Roberts, departed LAX on the morning of October 30.

Chapter 30

The rhythmic muffled thunk of the knife on the board-turned-kitchen-counter provided mindless cathartic exercise. Bright orange slices of carrot toppled and rolled on the wood, and a few fell to the sand near Lilly's feet. It was Halloween. The kids were fashioning costumes from every imaginable piece of flotsam the ocean deposited on their beach with each tide, a twice-daily visit from a generous benefactor. That was the rule. They could celebrate Halloween, but they had to make their costumes, and the materials had to be found, not bought. The tradition began when they moved to the island, mostly because Lilly couldn't get away with that idea when they lived in the States. The kids would have been mortified. They had moved to Tucson in the month of October, and Lilly had to buy all three of their costumes, whether or not she agreed with the philosophy. It was too embarrassing for the kids to make costumes when everyone else appeared as the current hot celebrity or cartoon. Mindless consumerism was now a distant memory. Finding clothes was a challenge, let alone costumes.

The kids had more fun making the costumes than they did wearing them, and the islanders made a fuss over them. It caught on with the other kids in the neighborhood. Last year, an impromptu party on the beach followed the creation of the costumes, and the entire village had participated. This year, advanced preparations fueled the frenzy. Today was the beach party, and the stricken village was a flurry of activity. A celebration was just what everyone needed.

She would be lucky if she could get the kids to eat before the party started. Amos, Sherri and Evie sat in the back of the tent, stringing together pieces of garbage and drift wood, arguing about what should go where. Lilly smiled. Finally – an evening to look forward to, even without Jean.

He had been gone three weeks. Lilly had expected it to take this long, but waiting much longer would be agony. She had adopted Henry's advice as her new mantra.

He can do anything.

She believed it, but fear threatened to devour her confidence. Jean could do just about anything, but he couldn't control the world. Maybe the authorities had dropped the case. The detective who had driven her to the airport all those months ago and a world away had had no idea who Jean was, or they would've caught him then. As far as they knew, Jean LaChance was anonymous in the United States, and now his name was Pierre LaPorte. Everyone on the island knew him as Mr. Pierre. Only Lilly called him Jean.

The tent flap flipped open, and Henry's bronze face appeared in the gap. A huge piece of netting dragged parallel lines through the sand behind him, erasing his bare footprints.

"Hi Mom," he said softly.

She looked up and smiled.

"What's that?" she asked

"Just a net. We're going to make Amos a sea monster. We have to get some sea grass to string through the net, so he might stink after the party."

Lilly laughed. "You guys might have to sleep outside."

"Could we? I like sleeping on the beach."

"It might be a good night for it."

Island life was ultimate luxury. The only danger was the ocean, which was a constant worry. But the people were honorable, and her kids were growing up carefree, trusting of those around them. Everyone knew who they were and where they lived. Jean had chosen the right place.

"Be sure to take a blanket. It gets cold in the middle of the night."

"Cool. Can me and Amos do that?"

"Sure."

She turned to him. Her mouth opened to correct his grammar, then remembered Jean's advice and chose other words.

"Where were you today?"

"I went fishing with Marcos. He has a great boat. He's teaching me how to drive it and all the best places to fish. We went way around to the backside, kinda where you and Dad got married."

Dad. There it was again. He was on everyone's minds.

Death of the Frenchman

Henry put his hand on his mother's shoulder. He was almost as tall as Lilly, even though he was a small kid. His quick hand whisked a few of the carrot slices, which he popped into his mouth. She turned and focused on his face. Henry's face had always looked like an adult's, especially after his father left. Henry had only been eight years old. He had assumed a man's role then, watching his younger siblings, fixing broken appliances with no knowledge, counseling Lilly with the skill of a therapist with his child's reasoning. Her prize. She swept a disobedient dreadlock away from his eyes.

"You look like your father," she said.

"Don't want to hear about him, Mom." The tone snapped from his lips.

Lilly looked back down at the carrots.

"I was talking about Jean."

"Oh." Henry paused. "That's different. Really?"

He tilted his head.

"How could I look like him?"

Lilly burst into laughter and Henry grinned.

"I don't know, that's the weird part. I guess you two are just connected. You think alike, you're both quiet. I guess you just started looking alike to me."

"Evie looks like Dad."

"I know; I see it too. Jean is worried she's going to look too much like him."

"I know. It's funny, isn't it?"

"At least she didn't get his nose, huh?" Lilly asked.

They shared a giggle. Jean had a long, sloping beak that looked quite regal on him, but every once in a while, if they really examined it, the nose was comical. Lilly's laugh wound down to a stop, and she let out a long breath.

"He's coming back soon, Mom," Henry said.

"I know. I know. I'm just worried, and . . ."

"You worry too much. Stuff like that takes time. It takes time to get there, to set it up, to get around. He'll be back, Mom."

Lilly looked into his face.

"You're right. I'm just anxious for him to come home."

"We all are. He'll be back soon."

Suddenly, he was done talking. Just like Jean. He hoisted the net and carried it to the back of the tent. Whoops and screeches came from the others when they saw the trophy. Amos jumped to his feet, plunged his arms through the net and assumed the posture of a sea monster; he roared around the other kids, stomping his feet and grabbing for them with out-stretched arms. Evie squealed. Even as a monster, Amos wasn't scary to her. Lilly left her chore and joined the kids, rolling around now on the tent's sandy floor, rescuing the maidens from the sea monster. Their bodies became a twisted mass of arms and legs. Laughter filled the tight canvas space. It went on for some time, until they were gasping for breath.

A throat cleared loudly over the chaos of family insanity. All heads whipped around and took in the sight of Jean, his face a mischievous grin, standing inside the tent watching them.

It was like someone hit a mute button. For several seconds, no one moved.

"Daddy!" Sherri screamed, and the entire family moved their scrum to envelope the Frenchman. A flurry of kisses and hugs ensued, the wild chatter a loud, incomprehensible static. The kids finally fell off a bit, and Lilly and Jean faced each other.

"Mon cheri," he said, lifting her hand and kissing it gently.

"Oh, God, I missed you."

Jean grabbed her and picked her feet off the ground, planting a long, deep kiss on her mouth while the kids groaned and made monkey noises. They parted, and Jean dipped Lilly deep to the ground. Lilly was crying.

"Why are you crying?" he teased.

"I just . . . just couldn't wait for you to come home," she managed.

"You know that I'll always come back to you."

The kids were pinned in so close to them they could hardly move. Lilly finally had had enough. She wanted him alone.

"Okay, kids, get your costumes and go outside! We have to get ready for the party. Give us a little time and come back in . . . in . . ." She looked at Jean, who shrugged his shoulders. Mom was in charge. "Half an hour. Now go."

The three older kids all groaned in chorus, and begrudgingly picked up their home-made costumes and dragged them outside the tent flap. Henry led them down the street just far enough to allow a moment of spousal reunion.

Lilly and Jean sat slowly at the table and looked at each other for minutes. Wordless conversation passed between them through the air separating their faces. Jean lifted his hand, palm facing her, and she interlaced her fingers in his, and gripped until they turned white. She had to touch him to believe he was actually home. Suddenly, the excruciating wait was over. The relief flooded out of her with tears that spilled over her bottom lids, and he leaned forward and kissed them off of her cheeks. After several minutes, Lilly spoke, knowing Jean would wait for her.

"How did it go?" she asked.

"It went fine. I'm here, yes?"

"Yes, but how did it go? Did you have any problems? Did you see anyone? Did we . . . did we get the money?"

"Most of it." Jean dropped his head.

Lilly was trying to gather unspoken information from his eyes, but his stoic manner was buttoned tight. A certain part of him had gone away, but she was gambling it would come back.

"Was it safe?" she asked.

"Most of it."

Lilly stiffened in her seat.

"Something happened, didn't it? What is this 'most of it' stuff? Are you going to tell me or not?"

He took a deep breath and scratched his head. He took both her hands in his, and brought them up to kiss them.

"First of all, I want to tell you that I missed you every day. Every day, all day. I wanted to talk to you every day. There is no question about this here, Lilly, and you should remember that. You have to trust me. That's the first thing."

"Okay. I trust you. What's the second thing?"

She was getting angry. Something had gone wrong.

"The second thing . . . is that you were right. They were ready for me. There's been some investigative work going on since we left the U.S. Remember Santino? The detective?"

Lilly's eyes were frozen with fear. She nodded her head.

"Santino stayed on the case, even after we left. They got my ID, somehow. Probably prints. They knew who they were looking for, evidently had a photo, and one officer at a bank must have confirmed the identity from that day I moved the money. They were waiting for me. You were right."

"Oh my God . . ."

"Wait, Lilly, I'm not finished." He paused. "They picked me up at the last bank and I woke up in a cell. It was pretty frightening. That's only the second time I've been arrested. Santino was there—he asked about you and the kids. I didn't tell him anything. Then, later that night, I got a chance to . . . to get out, and I took it, and it . . . anyway, I'm here. But the bad news is – they know who I am now and that I was there. That was a little . . ."

"Humbling? You think?" Lilly shot back. Her eyes were wild.

"Yes, humbling—that's the perfect word."

He waited for more backlash, having watched her face turn white, then bright red while he delivered his news. Lilly was still watching his face, chewing on the inside of her mouth.

"And?"

"And . . . what?"

"And are they on their way here right now, chasing you down, put you in cuffs, lock you up again?"

She was shaking from the story presented in cryptic bits.

"No, no Lilly. That was days ago. It was in Tucson. I went then to L.A. and spent a couple of days preparing so I could get out clean. It's okay now, I promise. They're still looking for me there."

"How do you know? Your face might be all over Venezuelan television. Technology is pretty good now, Jean. They might know exactly where you are right now and just wanted you to get to me and the kids; get you off your guard. You don't know exactly, do you?"

The inference burned. That he didn't know what he was doing. Her point was well taken, but her fear was inviting panic through the door.

"No, I don't know. What, why do you question me?"

LaChance had never used harsh words with Lilly. But instead of interrogation, he had hoped for a loving, sex-filled homecoming. Interrogation was for cops.

"What? Question you? Were you right about going? I can't believe how lucky you were, Jean. That could have been bad, really bad."

His face went flat. His eyes were steel. He dropped her hands and stood up from the chair.

"It was bad, Lilly." His tone was dark, the words, hissed. "I'm going to see my kids."

"Jean," Lilly said. "Jean, please . . ."

But he was out the tent flap and down the street. Lilly's guilt for her words seared into her brain. She didn't understand this part of the man she had married.

She stood slowly and pushed the flap to the side. From here, she could just see the heart-warming reunion of father and children. The kids jumped him and clung to him like cicadas. He hoisted Evie onto his shoulders and Lilly saw him wince with pain. They turned toward the beach and soon were out of sight.

Lilly turned and sat down on the bed corner. God, this was terrible. He had been locked up? The panic once again rose in her chest. Jean had attempted to play it down, but it had to have been awful; awful for him, awful to make that escape, awful to think about what would happen to them if he didn't. She shamed herself out loud.

A little bag of makeup lived in the top drawer of one of the bureaus rescued from the wreckage of their house. Lilly grabbed it and applied just enough eye shadow and mascara to enhance her femininity. She ran a brush through her curls and then fluffed her hair. She pulled off her T-shirt and chose a tank top that was a touch tight. It was one he liked. Afterward, she looked at her eyes deeply in the mirror.

She had a decision to make. She was angry about the whole Tucson affair. She was angry that he had left and even angrier he had been caught, for both of them. Two years of secure family life had covered her world with rose petals. Jean was a wonderful father and husband. The Jean she didn't know had been a thief for forty years. There was no contest. She had to get to know his alter ego.

They were down at the beach up to their waists splashing in the surf. Evie rode on Jean's shoulders high above the water, but all of them were soaking wet. The girls' shrieks overran the boys' laughter. Jean twirled like a danseur in the crashing waves. Lilly sat down in the sand and simply watched. She had earned the role of observer instead of the glee of participant.

After a few minutes, one of the kids noticed her and shouted over the sound of the surf.

"Mom! Come on!"

Lilly shook her head and waved her hand. In response, Jean started to the beach, his long legs dragging behind him in the water. He lowered Evie to the ground when he hit the sand. Arms outstretched to his wife, he beckoned her to join them. A mime of push and pull followed without the clutter of words that might require an apology. Body language conveyed their mutual craving. Jean needed to lose himself inside her, and she was ready for it. He waltzed to her in the sand, took her hands and lifted her into his arms, hugging her tight to his wet body despite her protests. They danced to the water's edge and ahead into the crashing waves. Henry began the splashing, and soon all three kids were soaking the dancing couple. Jean got them out to their thighs in the surf, then, with perfect timing, toppled them both dramatically on to the coming wave and out of sight. The kids went crazy as Lilly and Jean bobbed to the surface, just their heads showing above the water.

Lilly looked back toward the sand to make sure Evie was alright. Amos was sitting beside her. They were digging a hole. It was amazing. Their life was, for all intents and purposes—perfect.

Jean dragged her into water over her head out beyond the breakers where he could still stand. The crests of the breaking waves gave them complete privacy every several seconds. He covered her face with a frenzy of kisses.

"Jean, I'm sorry."

"Shhh, shhh, shhh," he shushed her. Suddenly she felt her shorts being pulled off.

"What are you doing?"

"Shhh, shhh, shhh," he repeated. "No one can see, and if they can, so what?"

She sucked in a deep breath and let her head drop back to the surface of the water as he manipulated her weightless body. The past weeks had been lonely and tense for both of them. Privacy had been rare without a door to lock behind them. He needed the release of emotion that only Lilly could provide. He needed to feel whole again; the incident in Tucson had taken that away. The crashing surf drowned out the sound of the couple's frantic breathing, and the kids made their way out of the water to home.

Chapter 31

The photo of Lilly and the kids rode atop the mug shot of the twenty-something LaChance on Santino's passenger seat for the trip to L.A., like a serendipitous coupling of symbolic records. The chase might as well have been over. Though they now had the identification of Jean LaChance, Santino knew how brilliant he was. There was a chance they could pick the Frenchman up at some airport, but they had to look everywhere, and LaChance had only to get through one security check—a simple task for a veteran criminal. He would lie low, use an alias, and get out as soon as was safely possible.

His meeting with LaChance had been interesting. Waking up in a cell would cause panic in most men. LaChance had stayed in total control, even though Santino had roused him from his knock out. The Frenchman hadn't said a thing, except for his request for the time. It was clearly, in hindsight, a time frame to get away before the Feds arrived.

Though the photo of Lilly and the kids was small, it was of good enough quality to enlarge. The final cropped result was a close side view of the sailboat. Items on the deck allowed Santino to make a rough estimate of the length on the water line and the height of both masts. Further inquiry identified the make and model as a Pearson ketch, somewhere between thirty-six and forty-two feet. But how did one go about finding one particular boat? He could place an ad in a sailing magazine asking the whereabouts of the owner. In theory, it sounded like a good idea, but it might take a while.

He also considered that this little scrap of potential evidence could lead to a charge of obstruction if anyone discovered he had it. The lead was so weak, though, he was not sure it would matter to the authorities. Surely, no one but Santino cared so deeply about apprehending Jean LaChance. The Frenchman was his obsession, no one else's.

Santino placed the ad in Sail Magazine. It was simple. The enlarged photo of the boat was placed with an inset of the words Do you know this boat?, plus a contact number. No other information was necessary. Any mention of criminal activity might destroy leads. Some cruisers had to be running illegal items, not limited to guns or marijuana. He didn't care what the boaters had been up to, he simply wanted to know where they had been.

Santino cleaned up the files from the case, stayed in touch with the Feds in the event LaChance was found, and returned to his private investigator gig. He worked when he wanted, saw his kids as often as possible, and waited.

His fixation on LaChance had taken on new life. If LaChance was alone, they would never find him. French authorities had been foiled for close to forty years.

But he knew LaChance was not alone. He was living with Lilly Parsons and four children. A whole family. Kids required consistency, the same house, same town, same school. From what Santino knew of Lilly, she wouldn't be on the run. Not with a baby. LaChance had to have landed in one location. The photo suggested a warm place with sunshine, palm trees and beaches.

Every evening during supper, Santino studied the face of the young Frenchman as though the answer would suddenly leap from the photo. The shrewd eyes reminded him of a photo of a jaguar he had once seen that stuck in his brain. The cat was perched in the upper branches of a tree guarding his kill. Its tongue was frozen in mid-lick to the side of its mouth. The white chin was smeared with blood, giving it a maniacal appearance. But the eyes. Frightening was not the word. Danger could be felt through the lens. The eyes jumped from the page, as if in motion. Those were the kind of eyes LaChance had, at least when he was cornered. He was also smart, talented; the most challenging breed of nemesis.

Santino knew he would not rest until he found the man who had eluded him three times. He prepared himself mentally for the time required. It could take months, or even years, but he would find Jean LaChance.

Chapter 32

The Halloween party would be in full swing by the time dinner ended. As Lilly predicted, the kids barely ate. They knew candy waited on the beach, as well as fruit and fish and rice—whatever the islanders could produce in the wake of Stephanie. Though a month had passed since the storm, the island still suffered the effects of devastating damage, and the electricity would be down for some time. Flights were now arriving on a daily basis, along with some mail, so supplies were available. Remarkably, no lives had been lost. Hurricanes were simply part of the island's life, and the cisterns had reached full occupancy on that terrifying night.

Jean sat at the head of the small table and ate with relish, gazing around the table at his little army, full of compliments for Lilly's meal. Constant lively chatter filled the tent to its seams.

Lilly's heart was bursting. They had had sex in the water off the beach, not at all the slow ecstasy of their regular lovemaking. It had been racy and within full view. Anyone watching carefully would have known what was going on, but it added an ingredient of eroticism she had never experienced.

If the kids were aware of what had happened, they didn't let on. Lilly guessed that Henry might know. She looked over at the boy, sitting next to his adopted father, not saying much, but watching Jean's every move, afraid to lose sight of the man who was finally back in their fold. Amos and Evie were involved in some sort of food game that included counting the pieces of fruit in a bowl. Sherri was helping. She was thrilled with having a younger sibling who knew less than she did.

Lilly looked up at Jean, and found him staring at her with hungry desire. She dropped her eyes like a shy teenager. She made a face, and he responded by licking his lips. Life in the tent would prove to be more challenging than first expected.

She found herself squirming in her seat. She had to halt the telepathic foreplay and get the kids out as soon as possible.

They dressed Amos in his sea monster costume. Sherri became a jellyfish covered with clear plastic bags, and Henry was a human winch, which took some time. He had scavenged hundreds of feet of rope from the wrack line, which he wound onto his body from head to hips and finished it off with the proper winch handle found on the far shore. Evie was a baby. That served as her costume.

"Okay, be careful and have fun. I want you home in a couple of hours," Lilly said.

"Mommy, aren't you coming?" Sherri whined.

"No, your father and I have some things to talk about from his trip. We'll be right here."

Henry smiled.

"Things to talk about, huh?" He pushed Jean gently on the arm and stole a sneaky glance at this mother.

"Hey!" Lilly said. "Get going, you guys."

The kids filed out, with Amos dragging Evie by the hand. Henry brought up the rear.

"Have fun talking about those things you have to talk about," he said, and disappeared out the tent flap.

"Jeez," Lilly said.

"He's old enough," Jean answered.

"He's twelve years old!" Lilly snapped.

Jean embraced her from the rear. She could feel that he had been ready for a while.

"Didn't you know about this when you were that age?" He began kissing her neck and let his hands explore her body.

"Twelve? I don't think so."

"Well, you weren't as mature as Henry is."

"Probably . . ."

The word was lost in a kiss as she bent her neck back to receive his lips. He was prepared to take full advantage of their privacy. He steered Lilly to the bed, where he pushed her back playfully onto the mattress and proceeded to strip his T-shirt over his head. Her shorts came off in one quick motion with his fingers hooked through the belt loops.

They had rules in lovemaking—Jean's rules. Lilly was not allowed to undress herself. That was exclusively man's work, he said. Seated beside her, he ran his large hand up under her blouse and made unhurried figure eights across her chest. The excruciating slowness of his tempo made her squirm. He was a brilliant lover. His movements were slight but accurate and never included force. He played, she set the pace. He always spoke in French, and the effect was fantastic. He could have been reading the thesaurus for all she knew, but she guessed it was more.

LaChance had no inhibitions. Lilly's conventional upbringing made her shy in bed, but Jean had grown up in the streets. His early encounters were most likely with hookers, though he never shared his past. He did anything and everything to give her pleasure. At first, it had been embarrassing, but Lilly got used to it quickly and waited every time for some new technique Jean had dreamed up. He took his leisure, sending her again and again into new heights of sensation, until she was exhausted. He was, as she had said, a professional.

After an hour of sweaty ecstasy, they lay back against the pillows on the bed, his fingers wound through her hair. The hurricane lamp on the table threw muted shadows over the white sides of the tent. Vibrant music from the party outside drifted in through the night air.

Jean reached over, produced a pack of cigarettes from his pants pocket and offered her one.

"You're smoking?" she asked.

"I've done a few things lately that I haven't done in a while."

She declined. He lit the smoke and threw his free arm up over his head, wincing with pain at the effort.

"How is your shoulder?"

"Still a little sore. I'm not the man I used to be."

"That's what you think."

Jean laughed.

"Was that good, my love?"

"Jesus."

"I missed our lovemaking."

"So did I."

They listened for a bit in silence to the revelry from the beach. Lilly broke the silence, unwilling to wait another minute.

"Jean?"

"Hmmm."

"Is everything okay? I mean, is there anything we have to be careful about? Do they know where we are?"

"Not a chance," the man answered.

Cryptic. Lilly was constantly interpreting his unspoken dialog.

"The mail is arriving daily now," he said. "I have to go find a phone and contact my friend in Los Angeles. He can start sending the money. Ramón says we can take his boat the next island over and get supplies. It'll take a while, but we can start to rebuild. I want your ideas on the house, the guest house, everything."

"Mmmm, that'll be good. It will give us something to look forward to."

"It will give us some privacy."

"That, too," she laughed. "This will be challenging, all of us in this tent."

"There's always the beach," he teased. "Most nights the beach is deserted."

"That's true."

"We should go," he said and got up from the bed. She watched his nude body stretch in the light from the lantern.

"Why?"

"We should go," he repeated. "There are people I would like to see."

Lilly rose obediently and dressed in the low light. Jean was waiting outside the tent flap, cigarette held in one hand, his face lifted to the tropical night sky. She wound an arm around his waist, and they walked toward the noise of the party, full of future dreams.

Chapter 33

The days ticked by in a long steady rhythm for Santino. New business was constant, mostly missing persons and jealous husbands or wives more than willing to trade money for any speck of dirt on an unfaithful spouse. He delivered, and the money rolled in. The tools of his trade increasingly depended on the burgeoning Internet, which expanded on a daily basis and held endless quantities of information that made his job easier. There was always the chance that the Internet would eventually make his services obsolete, but that might not happen for years. In the meantime, he squirreled away the money made from his new trade and lived comfortably on his retirement.

His kids were now in high school, and he spent almost every weekend with them. Each day with them was a constant reminder of how negligent he had been when they were small, when his marriage was intact, when he hadn't known the difference between a good marriage and a bad one. His ex-wife was friendly and accepting. They were becoming reacquainted on a basis that was satisfactory to both. Several times when they were alone, he had caught her flirting, and chose to ignore the danger that represented. Nothing good could come of a slip-up like rekindling a flame with an ex currently hitched to someone else's wagon.

Months passed. He ran the sailboat photo in every issue of several magazines with no results. A couple of calls had come in, but the boats the callers identified were living in a northern location, and had been for some time. The photo clearly had been taken in a warm climate. Santino could see palm trees in the background, and a white beach that couldn't exist anywhere north of Florida. Perhaps it was impossible. The more time that elapsed, the more discouraged Santino became. By now the photo was at least a year old. Cruisers moved constantly, sometimes on a daily basis. The clues in the photo cooled as the days flew.

He used his spare time to consider his quarry. He had read the reports from the French police over and over, hoping to uncover some new snippet of information. That LaChance was a professional was a foregone conclusion. He had almost no associates who could be identified, no close friends, no family. Until now.

The whole scenario with Lilly and the kids was puzzling. What would possess a brilliant career criminal to abandon his entire history to hook up with a ready-made family of four—recently increased to five? It was a good cover, Santino had to admit. It was also a lot of responsibility and a total life change for a loner like LaChance. It was possible they were so in love that the metamorphosis was worth it. But four kids? Santino had gone the other direction, not without regrets, but it didn't make much sense. The prospective love story ate at Santino's gut. He was jealous of LaChance, of Lilly, of the whole damn set-up.

It was also possible that LaChance was simply done with a life of crime. He was over fifty. His profession was a young man's game. Perhaps after years of deception and running, the man was just tired and ready for a life he had missed. If he had played it right, he probably had plenty of money.

Mid-life often brought peculiar makeovers.

Santino was also developing an odd kinship for LaChance that he couldn't set right. Santino's recent road to retirement had given him a renewed revulsion for the filth permeating the government. The department had leaned heavily on him. They had attempted to trade Santino's retirement for the capture of Prescott's thief. The way he looked at it, he was lucky to get out with what he had coming. He looked back with fresh eyes once he had cast off the paranoia of a system rife with favors and revenge.

LaChance became an unforeseen obsession. Just the memory of the man in an orange jumpsuit, injured, behind bars was enough to feed the manic fire. To anyone standing on the free side of those bars, LaChance was out of action. Santino had wanted to feel that. But the Frenchman had offered none of the satisfaction of a caged criminal. He had sat, smoked the cigarette that Santino had thrown him, and looked at Santino with no more regard than a stray dog. His body language was relaxed, yet taut, like a predator readying itself to jump an easy prey. The strength was captivating. He was beginning to like LaChance. Certainly he envied him. The two emotions were rapidly converging.

Santino contacted Evelyn Murray. Evelyn had no idea where they were, had not heard from Lilly since the post card from Tucson two years before. She didn't mention the money, and Santino wasn't sure how to broach the subject. Certainly, there could be other dead relatives in the picture that would explain the windfall.

After a particularly good payday, Santino had treated himself to dinner and a couple of beers with his former partner, Jose. It had been a long time, and they had lots of catching up to do.

Jose still worked for the LAPD. Hearing the changes in the department reinforced Santino's decision to retire. They talked about the LaChance case with the recent details filled in by Santino. The beers flowed freely, and Santino had to brace himself on both walls of his apartment entrance to free his feet from his shoes. The answering machine blinked the compelling greeting of new news.

He hit the button and peeled his clothes off one piece at a time.

"Mr. Santino, this is Sara Robertson. The photo of the boat posted in Sail Magazine belongs to me and my husband. We've just returned from cruising the Caribbean for two years, and saw the photo in the newest issue of the magazine. The boat is currently in Oriental, North Carolina. We can't imagine what this is about, but we're a little concerned. Please give us a call as soon as you get this message."

Sara left a number on the end of her message. Santino sat down heavily on the floor and blinked at the answering machine. He glanced at his watch, but it was well after eleven on the West Coast, which could be the middle of the night on the East Coast, if they lived anywhere near Oriental, North Carolina.

He was drunk enough to know that today was over, and it had already been four months since he had first placed the ad. One more day wouldn't make any difference.

As he fell into bed, a last thought ran through Santino's head. He was one more step closer to finding Jean LaChance.

Chapter 34

Henry stood at the bottom of the block-and-tackle adjacent to the foundation of the new house. The net on the rig held a bundle of two-by-fours destined for the roof. The men at the top, villagers hungry for income after the monster storm, nailed the boards in with machine precision; two men on a board, ten penny nails projecting from their teeth, working back and forth on the length of each board, pounding in rhythm. The roof grew as they watched. Up above on the peak, Jean supervised the workforce, shouting words of encouragement, joking when appropriate, enjoying the efficiency of many hands.

The groundbreaking ceremony was held the day after Christmas; a warm, breezy day with a cobalt sky free of clouds. Lilly ordered three bottles of French champagne from Margaret at the Hot Spot. With shovels in hand and a backhoe idling to the side, Jean and his neighbors bit into the Earth to begin rebuilding their lives. All the hired men were present for the ceremony. All brought shovels from home. Lilly pointed the camera while men, plus Henry, kicked their blades into the soil and smiled broadly for the photo shoot. Plastic cups of champagne were poured around, and immediately, construction began. They had laid the frame for the foundation in one day, mixed and poured the cement in two, and began framing the following week. The vertical construction followed; hundreds of cement blocks shipped from the Venezuelan coast were trucked to the house site, where the men carried them one by one to the foundation, cementing each in place.

Lilly had designed the house; bathrooms in convenient location, bedrooms for each of the boys and one for the girls, a veranda open to the ocean side looking over the village, a gravity fed shower with double heads, a kitchen adjacent to the veranda with an island, huge double sink and half-walls overlooking the same distant ocean view. On the second floor, the master bedroom was secluded on one side of the house, separated from the kids' rooms by a common space that housed an office and sitting room. A shop in the back of the house was designed for Jean and Henry, and the remaining space was dedicated to storage.

Henry worked alongside the men, and proved very valuable with his monkey-like ladder skills. He fetched tools and materials and watched the men's every move. He was a natural. The men enjoyed his company and youth and teased him mercilessly about his lengthening dreadlocks. Much like Samson's hair, no one would be allowed to cut it. Henry flourished on the banter from men who loved him.

Lilly walked the half mile from the tent three times every day: once mid-morning to bring drinks and fruit, once at noon lugging lunch for the hungry crew, and again in mid-afternoon for the break with more drinks and muffins or cookies. Food and drink became a full-time job. Sherri sometimes accompanied her, but Evie needed care. Amos became the abandoned babysitter.

The renovation attained a blinding pace, and each time Lilly climbed the hill from the village, she could see the difference, and photo-recorded the progress. They had followed all the hurricane codes in the construction, which also guaranteed resale value.

Evie changed daily. She was a strong child, full of vinegar, and adored Amos. He carted her around the village, introducing her to new life experiences. The villagers fawned over her, and she grew to expect attention and love with grace.

Lilly was thankful for the independence from motherhood. When Evie was hungry or upset, it was Amos she sought, and the boy showed a natural gift for mothering the child. The three older ones were largely on their own, immersed in island life. Except for the color of skin and hair, their movements and language were inseparable from the other kids.

Amos and Evie shared a special language unique to them; a strange mix of Spanish and English with a smattering of indiscernible words of their own creation. Lilly had worried about Amos for years. He was such an easy child, quiet and observant. Henry had been their leader before Jean came into their lives, and Amos simply followed his direction. Now, at ten years old, Amos took on the responsibility of a parent. No one had imposed this new role. As with everything, Amos slid into his task without question or struggle, and Lilly simply allowed it to happen. The first day they had returned home with the new baby, Amos had sat vigil for hours, finally falling asleep at the side of the crib. He was Evie's guardian angel.

Death of the Frenchman

Jean returned to the tent after dark most evenings, heading straight to the shower before often dozing over dinner. His body grew lean and muscular from the physical labor, his skin tanned bronze down to his waist from the Caribbean sun. His hair grew long and sprouted blond highlights. Lilly was turned on by his new look, but during the construction of the house, Jean was too tired at the end of each day for anything but sleep. Every several weeks, he took a day off to rest, and he and Lilly would jump in the Jeep and drive to a secluded beach or into the hills with a blanket and a picnic lunch to enjoy the privileges of married life. Lilly loved these days.

It was a marvelous time of all their lives.

Every day was consumed with the music of falling hammers across the island. Reconstruction was the primary focus, and all the residents were involved in some way. A landing craft owned by one of the island businessmen came into full use, making the daily run to a neighboring island twenty miles away to haul supplies and materials. The money went around and around, those with some sharing with those who had lost everything. Jean became a key employer. Most of the men were skilled in construction, and his crew varied from day to day as the workers showed up to make a day's pay to begin rebuilding their own homes destroyed by Stephanie.

In several weeks, Richard Prescott's cash began to arrive in separate packages from L.A. Although no one in their Caribbean world was aware of LaChance's past life, they suspected without judgment that something not completely legitimate had brought hard currency to the island. Not that they cared about legalities. Many islanders had been involved in illegal commerce just to survive. They knew that Pierre LaPorte was a good neighbor and friend, paid generously for their services and had a reputation of giving to those in particular need.

Jean considered this new-found magnanimous behavior payment for his former life of crime. Utilizing Prescott's disposable cash to rebuild their island made perfect sense. Everyone pooled their efforts, their money and resources, and the village that had been wiped off the face of the Earth slowly grew again into a village.

On the rare occasion that LaChance was able to spend some time alone, he walked the beach or drove the back roads, pondering what his life had become. Like a butterfly, he had undergone complete metamorphosis from Jean LaChance, infamous thief, to Pierre LaPorte, husband, father, community leader.

The two men could not have been any different.

LaChance had been cool, unbreakable, unconcerned with anyone but himself. He owned nothing, had no close friends, no social contacts apart from physical trysts with women for money, carried a gun and occupied an underworld existence that exiled him from main-stream society.

LaPorte was understanding and generous, the proprietor of a guest house known for its hospitality. Lilly was his wife and sole lover, and he showered her with all of his affection. The men on the island had become close friends and allies. Though he was foreign, he was absorbed into the community like a brother.

His new life was comfortable. He loved his family with a passion he couldn't have imagined in his past. Evie especially occupied his heart, and had cemented the conclusion of his past life. Every day they shared some special time, time he knew could run away without a thought. The three other children had become his family as well, had even taken the name LaPorte, though the adoptions were never legitimized.

Shadows also accompanied his solo detours. Though Lilly and the kids had given him a new life, there was a loss of history he was not able to resolve, a grief he could not shake. The trip to Tucson had been an effort to resurrect LaChance, to once again feel the rush of success that accompanied crime. His ego smacked with the fact that his very last job had been a failure. The guilt of lying to Lilly was suffocating. While Prescott's cash came in handy in their efforts to rebuild, LaChance had been stashing money for forty years. Secure accounts held much more than the Tucson banks safe-deposit boxes. In the end, he had been apprehended by the law. Behind bars, desperation had taken over his psyche, had almost derailed him.

He had been lucky. But the trip, the risk, had not been worth it. Before Tucson, he was a distant focus of authorities across the ocean. He was currently a wanted man in the States, a country geographically very near to his new existence. Though it was possible they would be safe here, there was always the chance that authorities would not give up until he was behind bars, or dead.

One of his calls to Dominic from a neighboring island included a request for the gun he had left in his friend's care. Jean had picked up the package at the airport and driven out onto a deserted inland dead end road to open the box and hoist the weighty weapon into his hand. Dominic had included plenty of ammunition. Just the possession of the weapon added a level of safety important to the old Jean LaChance. It also gave him a connection with his past that filled the perplexing void. He hid the gun at the new house construction so Lilly or the kids would not discover it by mistake.

LaChance was wise to be concerned. Santino had just made contact with Sara Robertson, the owner of the sailboat in the photograph.

Chapter 35

The Boeing Airbus landed in Raleigh, North Carolina in early afternoon. Santino quickly rented a car and was on the road within the hour. Greenville, North Carolina was less than a two hour drive, and Santino pushed the rental, once again feeling giddy with the chase. The magazine ad had finally paid off, though it had been six months since he first ran it. The month was May, three years since Lilly Parsons and her kids had disappeared.

Sara Robertson was quite sure the boat in the photo was theirs. She confirmed on the phone that they had flown a Jolly Roger for the cocktail hour every afternoon when not in transit, but then, a lot of cruisers did the same thing, she said. The boat was a Pearson 37, a dark blue ketch with two masts. They had recently returned from a cruising trip to the Caribbean, had been gone for eighteen months, and Sara was anxious to talk about the trip to anyone who might be interested. Santino wasn't. He thanked her graciously, took their address and asked if he could make a visit to their house, perhaps tomorrow?

"What is this concerning, Mr. Santino?"

"I'm on a missing person's case," Santino explained. "It's confidential, but I'm sure you could shed some light on the whereabouts of some people in the photograph."

Sara asked for his credentials, explaining that she would follow up on his information, just to make sure. Santino encouraged her to do so, and to contact the LAPD for confirmation.

"The LAPD?" She tried to hide her shock. "You're in Los Angeles?"

"Yes, ma'am."

"This must be an important case."

You have no idea, thought Santino, but what he said was, "Well, Mrs. Robertson, some family members have solicited my services. I believe it's a matter of personal interest."

"Of course," Sara said. "Well, we'll expect you tomorrow then. Please call us when you're on your way. We'll be home."

Santino thanked her and hung up.

So LaChance was hiding out in the Caribbean. Not a bad gig. The area was vast; there were lots of islands where someone with a less than a legitimate record could get lost easily. LaChance certainly wasn't the first.

Though Santino was anxious to speak with the Robertsons, he sat back in the sedan seat and tried to enjoy the ride. He had never been to North Carolina. The rolling green hills and endless pine trees were different from the dry climate of southern California, and cheerful flowers painted the landscape with an endless array of colors. Traffic was much slower than southern Cal, and soon, he found himself relaxing into the pace.

He arrived in Greenville and asked directions to the house at the local police station. Bill answered the door too quickly after the ring of the bell. He had been waiting and had heard Santino's car drive up.

Nautical-themed photos and knick-knacks adorned the Robertson living room. Sara offered Santino a Dark and Stormy made with rum and ginger beer, which he accepted. It had been a long trip.

"How was your flight?"

"Just fine. This country is beautiful. I've never been to North Carolina."

"Oh, you'll have to stay a while. We could show you the boat. It's just over on the ICW near Belhaven. Oh, you'll have to spend some time here, Mr. Santino. You'll love it."

Her accent was comfortable, assuring. The Robertsons could have been models for the L.L.Bean catalog. Sara and Bill were smartly dressed in polo shirts and pressed khaki pants, sported cleanly cut hair with just the first wisps of gray. Probably had made plenty of money in engineering, medicine or the stock market, now retired and enjoying the benefits of their white-collar labor. They launched into a short rendition of their cruising voyage, and Santino knew he'd be stuck for hours if he didn't move the conversation along.

Sara offered Santino a second drink which he politely declined, and took the opportunity to produce the photograph from which the sailboat had been cropped. Sara took the photo from him while Bill went to the kitchen to make two more drinks.

"I'm looking for this family. I believe they live on the island where you were anchored in this photo. Would you happen to remember which one it was?" He wanted to make sure they got down to business that would require recalling chronological events before the sailors got into too much rum.

"This is interesting. Yes, that's our boat, for sure. I don't know," she said, taking Santino's magnifying glass to view the photo more closely. "It's just a beach. There are hundreds of beaches in the Caribbean that look so much like this one."

"Look at the kids. Perhaps you saw them there at some point."

Ice cubes rattled from the kitchen. Sara peered hard at the photo, shaking her head. "I don't know, Mr. Santino. That's our boat for sure, but the kids, hmmmm."

Bill appeared in the doorway with the glasses, handing one to his wife and gesturing for the photo. He, too, looked closely at the faces in the photo with the magnifying glass. Sara chattered on about this island and that one. Had he ever been cruising? It was the best. He should really consider buying a boat and going on a cruise in the Caribbean. It was life-changing. They were thinking of taking another cruise, maybe in a year or so. Santino listened patiently, but his eyes were on Bill, studying the photo.

"Sara, look at this kid," he said. "This kid here with the long hair. Didn't this kid come out to the boat with a fish? Remember, he was in a skiff, some sort of a Whaler or something, and he had a couple of big groupers that he was selling to the cruisers. Remember? We thought it was odd that the kid was white and spoke perfect English. He obviously wasn't a local."

Sara looked long at the photo.

"I don't know, when did that . . . oh yeah! That kid. He was a wild child. He had long hair, almost dreadlocks. Yes, yes, I remember him. He didn't say his name, did he?"

"No, he didn't say a name, just sold us the fish for a pretty good price, if I remember right. He was kind of shy and serious. All business."

"Which child was it?" Santino asked, beckoning for the photo.

"This one," Sara pointed out. "The oldest one."

Henry. Santino remembered the child well. Very protective of his mother, almost threatening.

"Was his name Henry?"

"No, I don't know. He never said his name."

"Do you happen to remember where you saw him?"

Sara looked at her husband, who lifted his eyes to the ceiling, searching for information.

"Honey, did you write that in the log?"

"No, no, I don't think so. But it was later on in the trip. It wasn't in the Bahamas, I'm sure. Not in Jamaica or the Dominican. It was later on, maybe half way through our trip. Probably somewhere in the BVIs, or closer to Martinique or St. Lucia. Somewhere near Venezuela."

The couple talked about it for some time, and finally decided they didn't know exactly where they had met Henry, but Santino had narrowed it down to a string of islands in the lower Caribbean. Sara produced a chart with their cruising route and listed the islands in order where they had stopped. After a few more stories, Santino glanced at his watch and excused himself. He wasn't in a social frame of mind. He left his card, just in case the Robertsons would recall details when the Jolly Roger wasn't flying.

Santino drove slowly back to Raleigh, watching the scenery past his hands propped on the steering wheel. What was next? He had a change of clothes, was carrying his passport and had nothing in particular on his calendar. His outgoing message at home could be changed remotely. Raleigh had an international airport, and he was closer to the Caribbean than he would be back in L.A.

Santino returned the car and found a departures board. There was a flight leaving for Santo Domingo in the Dominican Republic the following morning at six. He stood staring at the board mouthing the words Santo Domingo over and over to himself under his breath. It was something he had never done before. The image of Jean LaChance flashed through his mind. He walked to the desk and booked a flight.

Chapter 36

By May, the family had moved into the house, and Lilly was painting every day—cheerful pastel colors that made the cement walls disappear. The bedrooms were first, driven by the motivation of sleeping alone in a room with her husband.

Jean and Henry had already begun on the guest house set back from the house and to the side, with a view overlooking the village and out to the ocean. The footprint was much larger than the house, and construction, much slower. The number of men on Jean's crew had dropped off a bit now that the house was complete. They had poured the foundation and were currently working on the walls and the layout of the guestrooms. Lilly welcomed the proximity to the construction. The walk from the tent had eaten a lot of her time, and now that Jean was home, there was no reason to be close to the village.

Lilly still cooked all day to feed the crewmen and her family. She balanced the books and handled the ordering of supplies that Jean brought to her daily. They had burned through heaps of money in the reconstruction, but, he reminded her, it was important and what else could they do?

One particularly hot afternoon, Jean came back early from the guest house, saying he had sent the men home. It was simply too hot, and he needed a rest. The kids were ordered down to the beach with instructions to come back before dark, and Lilly packed a bottle of wine and some snacks along with a blanket. They headed the opposite way in the Jeep.

Their wedding beach was in a secretive spot on the sunset side of the island. Privacy was the only reason to travel that far from the village. While Lilly unpacked the bags from the Jeep, Jean stripped to his skin and dove into the warm blue water. He swam out a distance and turned over onto his back, staring at the endless roof of sky. Life was so good. And today, he was alone with his woman. He put his feet on the bottom and stood, the water just up to his waist. He beckoned her to the water. Lilly watched from the blanket on the beach. His bronze muscles were gorgeous. She couldn't remember when he had looked so handsome.

Pulling off her shirt, she strode into the water, splashing with her hands in a playful game of "I'm gonna getcha." LaChance watched her come. She was beautiful. Even after four children, her figure was alluring, and she could use it when she wanted to. As she approached him, she could see below the waterline that he was ready. She screeched as he reached out and pulled the straps of her suit down to her waist, exposing her white breasts to the warm afternoon sun. He pulled her off her feet into deeper water, working the suit down her body until it slipped off her legs which wrapped like a squid around his torso. Though he was an exquisite lover and would service her for hours if she was game, every now and then he would simply take her for his own immediate pleasure. Lilly didn't mind. The frenzy of the lovemaking was erotic. One hand grasped her buttocks and the other wrapped around her waist. She clasp her hands behind his neck. He drove like a wild animal, finally bursting over the precipice with a low male growl.

They floated, face to face in the water, kissing in a constant stream. Jean pushed her body away and supported her back until she floated to the top, both breasts exposed above the surface of the water like twin islands. As the sun dropped from the apex of the sky toward the horizon, the Frenchman pleasured his lady in the bath of warm Caribbean water.

Later, he lay on his back in the orange glow of the setting sun, his naked body stretched out long on the blanket. She slept soundly on his shoulder, a sarong draping her torso. His free hand held a cigarette which sent a thread-thin stream of smoke into the hush of afternoon air. The constant therapy of rebuilding their life had strengthened the injured shoulder. The pain was barely noticeable for a guy like LaChance.

Bliss surrounded the white sand beach, and LaChance realized he was happy. He had never thought about the concept of happiness. Life was just life, and you used what you were given. On the island, they were relatively wealthy. Though electricity had not yet been returned to much of the island, it would soon be restored, Ramón had told him. Once power was available, money was available. The Tucson money had created substantial cash flow for the construction. Jean paid his men daily, and paid them well.

Despite all this, nagging doubt about the Richard Prescott case ate at his conscience. He knew intuitively it wasn't over. Though he doubted that French authorities would bother following him, something about the man Santino was unsettling. Santino had followed him, and for a long time.

Lilly stirred and opened her eyes.

"Bon jour," he said, kissing her forehead.

"Bon jour," she answered. "What time is it?"

"Almost five. We should go. The kids are probably home from the beach."

"What a wonderful, lazy, perfect afternoon," Lilly said in the middle of a yawn.

"Back to work tomorrow," Jean said, sitting up.

She gazed at his nude body on the blanket. He was so comfortable with nudity, but then, he was French.

"Are you going to dress before we go back?"

"What if I didn't? Wouldn't the neighbors be surprised?"

She laughed.

"So would the kids."

Lilly squirmed her body down into the sand under the blanket. Jean lit another cigarette and offered her one. She nodded.

"You've done such a great job with the house. I can't believe you've never done that before."

"I had lots of help. These natives know what they're doing."

She took the cigarette from his hand.

"Jean?"

"Hmmmm?"

"I'm sorry that I didn't trust your judgment about Tucson. I've felt guilty about that ever since. I said some really horrible things, and I'm really sorry. It was just me. I get nervous."

"I love you, Lilly, and you were right about not going. I got really lucky. That could have gone very badly. I had one chance, and I took it, and everything worked out. But I was lucky."

"No, what I mean is, I have to trust you. You're the most capable, talented person I've ever met and I would do anything for you."

"Okay."

"Okay, what?"

He gestured with both hands to his lap. Lilly gasped and gave him a good slap. Jean threw back his head and roared. She was so fun. He lifted his hand and cupped her chin, kissing her softly on the lips.

"I love you, Lilly. You're the perfect woman. Don't worry about that. You said what you said, and you meant it at the time, and you were right about a lot of things. But Henry's right. You worry too much."

"He said that to you?"

Jean frowned. "All the time. He's worried about how much you worry." He flipped over onto his stomach. "Don't worry, mon cheri. Life is good, really good. Everything is okay now, and we're right on track. We'll be finished with the guest house in a couple of months, and we'll just go on, and on . . . and on."

He pinned her flat on the blanket with his arms and gave her a kiss that almost made her pass out. He was right. Jean jumped up and pulled on his clothes.

"Fast work."

"We have to go, woman. My kids are home alone."

He winked at her playfully, threw the bag over his shoulder and headed for the Jeep. She watched him walk the distance to the vehicle before standing to shake the blanket. Giddy. That was the word. She was absolutely giddy.

They may have felt differently if they knew right at that moment, Santino was landing in Santo Domingo.

Chapter 37

Santino pressed his neck against the head rest and fought to get comfortable in the hard seat of the prop plane. He had been on the hunt for three weeks, flying or taking boats from island to island, working his way from the Dominican Republic, through the BVIs, St. Lucia, St. Barts, Martinique and numerous small islands on the way to the Venezuelan coast. The trip had been lovely; warm, blue Caribbean water, white sand beaches, perfect palm trees. If he had had no agenda, it would have been a great vacation.

He had no hits at all. No one knew a Frenchman who had come in the past two years with a wife and four children. There were plenty of Frenchmen on the islands, and he met as many as he could, but no one could ID the man in the mug shot, or the children in Santino's photo.

Despite constant failure, Santino was having a marvelous time. Everyone he met shared a smile, was helpful and sincere. They bought him drinks and assisted him in finding places to stay, often at little or no charge. The children were wonderful, with no fear at all of the man who was foreign, they knew, but spoke their native language with a funny accent. It was uncanny. The sense of being at home in a foreign land.

Initially, he began his search at a frantic pace, staying only as long as necessary to determine they indeed weren't there. Soon, his journey developed a natural rhythm determined by scenery and culture. The farther he went, the slower he travelled, until he found himself spending several extra days on each island, reveling in the gorgeous tropical weather and the gentle company of the local people. The dirt of L.A., its vicious street life, crooked politicians and star worship that had defined and shaped his life was melting from his consciousness. A basic goodness of life was here, and the inclusive nature of the population was magnetic.

He began to understand why LaChance, former career criminal, would dump that existence for the life he now saw.

The small plane lurched suddenly and began a steady wobbling descent. Their destination loomed through his window. The island appeared to be around ten miles long, with some rocky relief, highlands, agricultural fields and a single, one-track village adjacent to a long white beach. A dirt airstrip barely long enough to accommodate the run-out of the prop plane occupied the highest point of land. The plane circled in low, the tires skimming the tops of the trees just seconds before touchdown. Suddenly, they had arrived.

Santino passed through the cement building vaguely resembling an airport, to stand on the road's end. A sign hanging from the square building across the road identified it as the Hot Spot. Unlikely it could be anything but a bar, and the time was right for a drink.

"Good afternoon, sir," Margaret said as he cleared the threshold. "What can I get for you?"

"Afternoon. A Red Stripe, please."

"Right away," Margaret said. Santino had developed a taste for the Jamaican beer that was a staple at every restaurant and bar in the Caribbean.

Ice clinging to the label fell onto the bar into a frosty pile and sent Santino's mouth to watering. He closed his eyes and took a long swig. How much longer could this go on? The chase was losing its purpose. He was losing his motivation.

"What brings you to our island?" Margaret asked.

"I'm actually looking for a friend from the past. We knew each other in Vietnam. He was in the French army. He . . . he saved my life, and we never saw each other again. I ran into another vet several months back who said that he was living in the Caribbean."

The compelling tale had been honed during the weeks of Santino's search.

"What is his name?"

"That's precisely the problem. I had terrible head injuries at the time, so I don't remember his name, but maybe if I hear it I would remember. I think he has children as well, and he's been living here for about two years."

"That could be Mr. Pierre."

"Mr. Pierre?"

"Well, Pierre LaPorte. We call him Mr. Pierre. He lives here with his wife and children. They have four children."

Her broad white smile glistened against the light from outside.

Santino lifted the beer to his lips to hide his excitement.

Death of the Frenchman

"Is his wife's name Lilly?"

"Yes, Lilly. That's it! What did you say your name was?"

Santino was familiar with the efficiency of the coconut telegraph, and wanted to reach LaChance before the news of his arrival did.

"My name is Guy. I would like to surprise him. Could you tell me where he lives?"

"Just a minute, please."

She went to the side door and yelled, "Phillip! Phillip! Take this man to Mr. Pierre's house, will you?" She was yelling at a taxi that didn't appear to have a driver. A head slowly emerged above the level of the backseat.

Santino left a ten dollar tip and kissed Margaret's hand with dramatic flourish. Phillip was scratching his head, bothered to be roused from his nap. But as soon as Santino sat down in the back seat, Phillip greeted him warmly. Santino would tip well.

The drive from the airstrip featured landscape that should have been exquisite. Extensive damage had transformed it into a war zone; trees were toppled and twisted, building materials, apparently from houses, were scattered like confetti on every field and caught in the tops of the trees still standing.

The sight of the wreckage magnified the emotion percolating in Santino's mind. Suddenly, he was in the right place, and would meet LaChance within minutes. Three weeks of hunting his prey without success had left him unprepared for the confrontation. What would he say? The vision of LaChance sitting like a caged jaguar in the cell in Tucson sprang into his head. Santino was alone. LaChance was a free man, probably armed. United with his family in his territory gave the Frenchman a distinct advantage, and would make him extremely dangerous. Sweat erupted from Santino's forehead. What the hell was he thinking? There was no time to back out. Two people on the island so far knew he was looking for LaChance, but that was enough. Word traveled like lightning in a community this size, where residents looked after each other with the loyalty of litter mates. Little else remained but to carry through and hope for the best. Santino had no idea what to do now that the situation was at hand.

The taxi started to turn into a narrow drive off the main road. Santino could just see a building under construction through the ragged trees. He lurched forward in the seat. "Stop here," he ordered. Phillip pulled the taxi to the side of the drive.

"Is that it?"

"Yes, that is Mr. Pierre's house."

"Thank you. This is good."

Santino pulled some folded bills out of his pocket and paid Phillip twice the fare. He climbed out of the car and hoisted his bag to his shoulder. The taxi backed up and turned around. He was alone. He quickly rifled through his bag for his handgun, which he pocketed. He turned toward the house.

Santino had pursued the French thief for over two years, never sure of what he would find when he caught up with his prey, but the scene in front of him was far from what he expected.

A cement block building with walls and a roofing frame stood a hundred yards ahead. Several men balanced like monkeys on the rafters, nailing on board after board. A steady rhythm of hammer blows echoed through the site, occasionally punctuated by short phrases from the men coordinating the effort. The men appeared local—small, native-looking guys with jet-black hair. But one man stood out among them. He was down on the ground below the roofers, on hands and knees playing with a baby in a white cotton dress. She was laughing and waving her arms, trying desperately to grab the man's nose, bubbling and cooing in her efforts. He gently teased her into shrieks, and the men on the roof laughed in response.

It was LaChance.

The Frenchman stood and swept the baby from the ground and cartwheeled her around in a circle. The little girl's shrill laugh echoed through the yard, and a dark-haired woman called loudly from the porch and ran out to the drive.

"Don't scare her," she cried, laughing nervously.

"She's fine. She loves it," LaChance answered. He grabbed the woman around the waist and kissed her. Santino stared at her face. The woman was Lilly.

At last. Here they were, lovers surrounded by the broken tropical landscape that had once been beautifully exotic, and would recover in time. Santino had heard stories of the destruction as he made his way from island to island, but this was the worst he had encountered so far. Ugly broken snags and gnarled twisted stems of unidentifiable vegetation enclosed the family complex. What must have been gorgeous at one time was now wreckage, and in its midst, LaChance and Lilly smooched like teenagers. They were lost in each other and the girl child between them.

Even at this distance, without being able to see their eyes, Santino could tell they were in love. In serious, life-long love holding a baby between them. A mental image of LaChance's face behind bars flashed in Santino's brain. The dead eyes. The hard face. The caged jaguar.

That was not this man. Not anymore.

Santino set his bag softly on the ground and turned toward the road. He walked back out the way the taxi had come and stood for several minutes out of sight of the building. He had to put this all together, and soon. His heart prickled with jealousy, pumping the adrenalin which surged through his system upon finally finding them. He stood for a long time at the side of the road corralling his emotions and suddenly realized he had lost sight of his errand. What could happen now? He could always walk to town and get a room and think about this overnight. But would tomorrow be any different from today? LaChance would soon find out he was here, and go looking for the American whose life he had not saved during the Vietnam War. There was only one thing to do.

Santino retrieved his bag from the drive and walked toward the house. As the construction site came into view, he saw that LaChance was back up on the roof working. Santino took in the complex; a beautiful yellow house with white-framed windows stood ahead, its deck overlooking the ocean far below past the island's village. To its right lay the building under construction. Seven men and a boy with long wild hair wielded hammers; nails protruding from their mouths and bulging their pockets. Movement drew Santino's eyes to the house, and Lilly emerged from the door with a pitcher and glasses on a tray. She saw Santino and jerked to a stop, jostling one of the glasses from the tray. It fell to the ground and exploded. Santino's gaze snapped up to the roof.

LaChance was looking in his direction. Santino repositioned his bag and walked the remaining distance to the building. He felt the eyes of the predator from above, ready to pounce. He kept his gaze to the ground. The back of his festive cotton shirt was soaked.

When he reached the building, he raised his eyes. LaChance was looking straight at him, a hammer gripped in his right hand. The carpenter's tool had suddenly taken on the look of a weapon.

"Mr. LaPorte!"

Hearing that address for the first time—everyone called Jean 'Mr. Pierre'—Henry hopped across the rafters to his father's side.

"Dad, isn't that the guy . . ."

"Yeah. Go in the house. Tell your mother to stay inside," he ordered. He turned to Henry and laid a hand on his shoulder. "It's okay, buddy. He's alone. I'm sure he just wants to talk."

LaChance's eyes swept to the road and beyond. Santino was alone. It was too weird. It was also a shock. Henry slid down the ladder stringers and hit the bottom at a run for the house. LaChance shouted to the crew that they were done for the day. Unlike Henry, he took his time. He reached the bottom of the ladder, turned and held up a hand to Santino to wait.

The workmen felt the tension at the arrival of the unexpected guest. They shouted back farewells but made no move to leave. Santino stood alone, facing the small native army of his nemesis' friends.

The Glock was hidden at the rear of the construction site in a concrete block. Lilly still didn't know it was there. LaChance retrieved it and checked the magazine, then pulled his shirttail free and stuck the gun into his waistband. He could almost hear his thumping heart. Hundreds of scenarios flew through his mind. Evidently, the man did not give up easily. The possibility of killing Santino right now was real.

He emerged from the front of the building, wiping his hands slowly on a rag. He looked steadily at Santino.

"Santino."

"Mr. LaPorte," Santino answered. He knew nothing good could come of blowing LaChance's identity. The move was respectful.

LaChance turned to the men and thanked them in Spanish, shaking hands all around, saying he would see them the next day.

The men started back toward the village reluctantly, swinging their hammers, turning periodically to look back to their friend. The two men stood together and watched them go. LaChance glanced over to the house, where Lilly and Henry stood inside the door, white fear in their faces. He waved and blew Lilly a kiss. He turned back to Santino without a word. His expression was lethal.

"As I said before, LaChance, you're a hard man to find."

LaChance gestured, palm up, toward the Jeep. The men climbed in, Jean at the wheel. The Jeep backed up and started down the drive. Lilly watched them in a panic from the doorway. She threw the screen door open and attempted to run after the Jeep. Henry grabbed her arm, which swung her around on the steps. She fell to her knees and burst into tears. Henry tried to comfort her.

"Mom, it's okay. They're only talking. Dad's gonna be fine."

A quiver in his voice betrayed the assurance he had hoped for. He was worried, too.

As the Jeep turned onto the main road, LaChance reached into his shirt pocket and produced a pack of Camels. The quick movement made Santino jump. LaChance smiled slightly. He gave the pack a sharp shake, and the cigarettes leapt half way out. He offered the pack without a word to the man in the passenger's seat. Santino hadn't smoked in a couple of years, but considered for a second that this might be his last one ever, like a prisoner at a firing squad. He took the cigarette and nodded. LaChance lifted the pack to his mouth and pulled a cigarette out with his teeth. He produced a lighter and handed it first to Santino. Their hands touched slightly in the exchange. LaChance drove back toward the airstrip and took a side road with a bad surface. Sweat rolled down Santino's back. Was this it? He felt in his pocket for the gun, wondering whether he would have to use it. LaChance could easily kill him and get away with it in this outback.

"I have to tell you, half a dozen people know exactly where I am and why I'm here. This will be the first place they look if they don't hear from me in a couple of days," Santino lied.

LaChance said nothing.

In fact, no one knew exactly where Santino was. It would take a while to retrace his erratic trail. The trip to the Caribbean had been spontaneous, unplanned.

The Jeep rounded a corner and came abruptly to the end of the road, where discarded beer cans and blackened pieces of firewood suggested a night-time teenage hangout. LaChance cranked the keys out of the ignition and climbed out quickly, pulling the gun out of his waistband in one motion. He faced the Investigator with level, hard eyes. He stood outside the Jeep, gun in hand, though not aimed at Santino, and waited. The entire trip had taken less than three minutes. From this distance, the discharge of the gun would be heard from the house. Jean was sure Lilly was waiting for something.

Santino grabbed the hand grip and stepped out of the Jeep in slow motion. He thought about the gun in his pocket. The two men faced each other, smoking in the still air of the tropical afternoon. Finally, LaChance finished his cigarette, threw it to the ground and flattened it under the toe of his boot. He shrugged his shoulders in a wordless question. Santino had called the meeting.

"You found a good place to land," Santino said.

"How did you find me?"

"I went back to Lilly's house in the desert. The photo you left had a sailboat in the background. It's taken me all this time to find the owner and retrace their steps. I've been all the way down from the Dominican."

LaChance raised his eyebrows. The guy was certainly persistent.

"You're a worthy opponent, LaChance. I have to say, that was quite an escape."

LaChance shrugged his shoulders again dismissively. "It's what I do."

"I can see that."

Still, neither moved. Santino finished his cigarette and dropped the butt on the ground and stepped on it. They stood facing each other in the unbalanced duel on opposite sides of the vehicle. The thick humid air twitched with expectation. Santino appeared to be unarmed, but that wasn't LaChance's biggest concern.

LaChance's life had always been full of options. Options to stay, to run, to take jobs or not, as he pleased. Family and a home had erased options. He wasn't going anywhere, and by his own choice. His only alternative was to kill Santino. In this community, he could get away with it. It could have been an old feud. No one here knew Santino, or what position he held. A body was easily disposed of in the vast stretch of blue water surrounding the island. He waited for Santino's next move.

"What now?" the Frenchman asked.

"I'm not sure, LaChance. The FBI knows who you are now. They gave quite an interesting slide show on your life. I have to say, I'm impressed. There are a lot of people who would like to meet up with you."

He shifted his gaze down to the gun.

"You're not a killer, LaChance."

"Not yet."

Santino was clearly nervous. LaChance doubted that anyone knew exactly where he was. If more men showed up, hiding out for a while to avoid capture would be possible, and the villagers would cover for him.

"Where's Prescott's money?" Santino asked.

"You saw the guest house, our house. The hurricane destroyed everything. The cash has mostly gone to reconstruction. It's in the villagers' pockets now. Good luck getting it back."

He paused and looked hard at Santino. "You're a persistent man. Not many cops would make the effort. That's good work."

It was a compliment. Santino shrugged.

"It's what I do."

Imitation being the highest form of flattery brought a flicker of a smile to the Frenchman's face. Santino caught it and smiled back. The two men faced each other; the thief armed with the deadly weapon, the former lawman at a disadvantage.

LaChance looked down at the Glock and bounced the weapon slightly in his hand.

"What were you thinking Santino? Arrive empty handed and corner me?"

"Oh, I brought a gun," Santino said. He put up both of his hands, palms facing LaChance, then reached slowly into his pocket and drew out the weapon, muzzle turned away. LaChance shifted the Glock straight at him.

"Make your choice Santino."

Santino opened both his palms and set the handgun down on the Jeep hood, then stepped back with his hands still up.

The mortal enemies stood on opposite sides of the hood, the Jeep's cooling engine ticking at maddeningly random intervals and jolting frazzled nerves. Caught in an impossible situation; both wanting desperately to avoid a killing. Small rivulets of sweat ran down their faces, and pesky flies buzzed around their heads, but neither man dared to move to shoo them away. The enormity of the destined meeting hung in the heavy tropical air. Each looked across to the other man, helpless to pass judgment on life from another perspective. Each struggled with the conflict of law and lawlessness, the battle of mutual respect and professional duty.

LaChance stood for some time with the gun pointing at Santino, then slowly lowered it to his side.

"Thank you," Santino said, and wiped his forehead with the back of his hand. "Jesus, it's hot here."

The edgy energy forced a chuckle from LaChance's throat. Seeing this, Santino laughed out loud, which brought the same response from the Frenchman. Every few seconds, they caught each other's eye, and the laughter began again, forcing its way past mistrust and power, finding its own place in the mad scene.

As both men struggled for composure, LaChance reached for the cigarettes, first offering one to Santino. Santino walked around the front of the vehicle and took it. LaChance held up the lighter and flicked the flame for him.

They were standing side by side. Santino bent his head to light the smoke and said, "Well, what the fuck do we do now?"

The abrupt burst of laughter startled a flock of parrots from the tree overhead in a screeching chorus that pierced the sultry air. Both men jumped in response, then glanced quickly at each other, unsure. The hilarity escalated and fell, then escalated once again in a roller coaster of nervous uncertainty and mistrust. The parrots were gone, their voices quiet. Finally, the men looked at each other, eyes calm and confident, a shadow of a smile written on both faces.

There would be no killing today.

LaChance turned around and sat down on the bumper of the Jeep. He dropped his head back and looked into the deepness of the sky. Santino joined him.

"I've been running all of my life, Santino," LaChance confessed. "I'm done. This is a good place. It's the only home I've ever had. You've finally found me, and the only option I have is to kill you."

He looked over at Santino.

"I would do it, too. You would be my first."

"I believe you."

"I know all it would take is a phone call. But I'm not leaving. I have a wife and four kids now, with the last name of LaPorte. LaChance is gone. That life is over."

The men sat in the quiet of the hot afternoon, side by side, smoking like chums on the front bumper of the Jeep. There was nothing to say, so they sat in silence enjoying the bizarre anti-climax. High above in the air, stenciled against the blue of the sky, two tropic birds twittered their song, sweeping tail feathers floating like streamers on the breeze. The tremolo injected peace into the tense atmosphere between two men on opposite sides of the law. Finally, LaChance stood and snuffed his cigarette.

"I could use a beer. You?"

Chapter 38

Phillip arrived at the house an hour after the men had left to relay a message to Lilly— Jean and Santino had gone for a drink at the Hot Spot, she and the kids should not hold dinner for them, that everything was fine.

That hour had been interminable torture for Lilly. She stood at the door with Phillip, peppering him with questions he could not answer. Yes, they had arrived at the Hot Spot, and yes, Mr. Pierre and his friend were sitting outside at a table drinking beer.

His friend?

Wasn't Santino the man who had threatened her and the kids back in Tucson months ago? Wasn't he the same man who had tirelessly pursued LaChance, even after his disappearance? She knew her husband well enough to trust his judgment, but in his absence as the hours ticked by and the sun slipped beneath the horizon, the anxiety grew to a level that left her pacing through the house, checking out the window every few minutes, frantic to tears.

She put the younger kids to bed at eight thirty, drank a glass of wine which then became two and then three, fighting panic that threatened to take over her psyche. Henry stayed up with his mother, unable to console her. He was worried, too. Santino was the man who had intimidated his mother, and had laid his hands on her in their kitchen in Tucson. Santino was also the man who had taken Lilly to the airport while the kids waited at the house for hours with his partner, Jose. Those hours closely resembled these hours of excruciating delay. He would never forget the face of that man.

Lilly watched the hands of the battery operated clock in the kitchen as they crept slowly in their never-ending circle, telling the story of only the passage of time, but not what was happening to the man she loved, now in the company of his adversary.

At ten o'clock, a car door slammed in the distance, shattering the quiet inside the house. Lilly rushed to the door. Beyond the flood of the kerosene lamp light, she could hear voices over the insect chatter, coming from the direction of the road shrouded in darkness. At first, her brain heard agitated male speech, then realized that while it was loud, the voices were not angry, but laughing.

"Is that singing?" Henry stood close by her shoulder.

He was right. From the direction of the road rose two men's voices, singing the Battle Hymn of the Republic. The first verse finished, and the chorus rose into the night sky, relaying the promise of Glory, glory, hallelujah, His truth is marching on! The second verse began, a slaughter of long-forgotten lyrics that crumbled into laughter and ended in a second chorus of Glory, hallelujah, His truth is marching on!

Lilly and Henry stood in shock on the porch step as the voices drew nearer, until two men, arms wrapped around each other for support, emerged into the pool of light thrown into the yard.

"Mom, I think they're drunk," Henry said.

"I guess so," Lilly answered. Her tone was furious.

"Lilly, my love," Jean yelled from the yard. "Meet Guy Santino, Private Eye."

"We've met," Santino said.

"Oh, yeah, that's right. Lilly, my love, how are you?"

LaChance freed himself from Santino and lurched up the steps to his bride. He threw his arms around her in a clumsy embrace and laid a boozy kiss on her mouth.

"You're drunk," she snapped.

"You're a smart woman," Jean answered.

Henry was standing to the side, a youthful smirk written across his face. He had never seen his father drunk. He was jealous. They looked like they were having fun.

Lilly pushed him away and turned into the house, but Jean was so loaded, he didn't recognize her dismissal. He turned back to Santino and was forced to catch himself on the railing. Santino took his extended hand. Together the men followed Lilly and Henry into the house, supporting each other through the door.

Lilly stood with her arms cinched across her chest on the far side of the table. Her inability to make any sense of the scene fed the anger boiling inside. Santino and Jean stood, arm in arm just inside the door, suddenly ashamed of their condition, failing in their attempt to hide their bad boy evening of fun. Santino pulled his arm from Jean's and approached Lilly around the table. He offered his hand in peace, which she ignored.

"Mrs. LaPorte, I'm very glad to make your acquaintance. I want to apologize for any discomfort I might have caused you in the past."

He stood swaying with his hand extended, waiting for the woman to make her choice. From the far side of the table, Jean spoke.

"Lilly, everything is okay. We have come to an agreement."

He stopped and sat down heavily in the nearest chair.

"Please, Lilly. Guy is our guest. I'm sorry for the worry. My love. Everything is okay now."

His eyes pleaded with futility. She looked away. He reached his hand toward her.

"Please Lilly, please."

He looked over at his son.

"Henry, tell your mother. Everything is okay now," he repeated.

Henry's eyes widened. He knew his mother, how long she could hold her anger. But the shocking scene of the men's return had assured him that his father had once again solved the biggest problem in their lives. It was the only thing that weighed on them. He touched his mother's arm.

"Mom," he said quietly, taking his father's lead. "Mom, shake his hand. Mr. Santino is our guest."

Lilly tightened her lips and offered her hand. Santino raised it to his face and kissed the back gently. His inebriated smile was warm and soft. Lilly gave in and smiled.

"Welcome to our home, Mr. Santino."

"Please, call me Guy."

"Guy."

Santino lowered Lilly's hand. She looked back to LaChance.

"Okay, explain," she said curtly. "What agreement have you come to? Why is everything okay now?"

"Because we're going to kill Jean LaChance," he answered. "Lilly, do we have any more wine?"

"What?"

"Wine."

"No, the other part. About killing Jean LaChance."

He smiled and blinked his eyes slowly.

"Please, Lilly, may I have a glass of wine? Then I'll tell you about killing LaChance. Santino, sit down."

Lilly looked over at Henry. "Time for bed, honey."

"No way!" Henry said, and grabbed the chair next to his father. He was thrilled with the direction of the conversation. Obviously, the men had come to a solution, and that solution included killing Jean LaChance. He had to hear this.

"No, no, Henry can stay," Jean said. He reached over and tousled the boy's hair. "My good boy," he said softly. Henry beamed. "Santino, have you ever seen hair like this on a white boy?"

Santino and Henry laughed. Lilly had turned her back to get the wine. Though still angry, the relief of seeing them arm in arm had made the ground drop from beneath her feet. The bottles of red wine in the rack stirred nostalgia soothing to her heart. It had connected Jean and Lilly on the porch of the house in the desert, where they first met. She breathed out a long sigh and poured three glasses, then paused and reached for a fourth from the cabinet. Henry was almost old enough.

The conversation at the table had taken a turn to a loving berating of Henry's hair. The men flanked him at the table and took turns touching his dreadlocks while the boy dodged their hands, giggling. Like an attentive waitress, Lilly set first Santino's glass, then Jean's, then a half-portion in front of her oldest child. His wide eyes took in the glass and slowly shifted to his mother's face.

"Thanks, Mom," he said shyly.

"I guess the order of the day is drinking, and honey, you deserve to join us."

LaChance raised his glass in a salubrious toast followed by Santino, then Lilly, and finally Henry. Glasses clinked together mid-table in the atmosphere of warm embrace. They drank through the hushed silence of the room, and Jean opened the conversation.

"Former LAPD Detective Santino has been chasing us for two years, as you know. He was the detective at the house the day after you left with the kids, Lilly. He spoke with your mother, traced you to Tucson, and, well, you remember, took you to the airport the day I left the city."

Santino turned his full attention to Lilly. "I'm so sorry, Lilly. We were after your husband, not you. I was doing my job. I guess that doesn't make it right."

Lilly pressed her lips together. "Well, no one suffered. The kids were okay. That was my only concern."

"Yes ma'am."

Jean continued. "Before I went back to Tucson to get the money, crack detective Santino here ran my prints and found my identity from an arrest when I was twenty. Interpol had them on record. They had my face, my name, everything but my location."

He looked at Lilly. "You were right, mon cheri. I walked right into it. They were ready for me."

He had not shared the information with Lilly until now, but proceeded with the story of his forceful capture, his meeting with Santino in jail, his escape from the cell, with the aid of junior Police Officer Knowles. As his tale unfolded, Lilly raised her hand to her mouth in horror.

"You came that close?" Lilly gasped.

Santino said, "If Jean hadn't gotten out that night, he would be in a French prison as we speak—for many years. It was maddening, his escape. It was also impressive," he said to Jean.

LaChance nodded. They clinked glasses again.

"But how did you find us here?" Lilly was confused.

"Ahhhh, yes, our sentimental criminal," Santino teased, and laughed. "He went back to your house in the desert, to reconnect, I guess."

"In part," Jean added. "I also had to leave you all behind." He looked at his wife, and his voice dropped to a whisper. "Lilly, I love you. Look at all that has happened since I met you. My name has changed, my life has changed. I am a completely different man. Before, I had no one, nothing. I am now Pierre LaPorte."

He said the name in a full French accent. Somehow, it sounded more convincing than the fake name she had come to know, but never used.

"I was a thief, Lilly. I know we never spoke about it, but you should know that. I stole other people's money. Other people's possessions. I never felt bad about it. I didn't care about anyone, didn't depend on anyone but myself. You met that man, Jean LaChance."

He was looking down at the table top, in an uncharacteristic moment of self-debasement. They sat silently. Lilly felt a clutch in her throat. Of course, she had never thought about him in quite that way.

He looked up.

"Going back to Tucson was never about the money, Lilly. This life is mine now, and I am my life. Everyone here," he gestured in a wide circle inclusive of the village and the island, "everyone knows me as Pierre LaPorte. This is who I am now. I went back to, to regain that man I was. I couldn't leave the identity yet. I had to prove to myself that I could be him again—that I could do it again, Lilly."

He leaned forward in his seat, his eyes pleading with her to understand.

"I needed to find him again, that's all. And part of that was to leave you behind, all of you," he glanced at Henry. "I had to leave you at the house where I met you."

He sat back abruptly in his seat, nearly spilling the wine in his hand.

"Little did I know Dick Tracy here would go back to the house."

"What?" Lilly asked.

"Yes, ma'am," Santino said. "I would never have found you except for the photo of you and the kids. There was a sailboat in the background, anchored off the beach. I found the boat in North Carolina. They were cruisers, here in this anchorage about a year ago. Henry, you sold them a fish. They remembered you."

"Really?" Henry's eyes were saucers. He was thrilled to be part of the story.

"Well, they remembered your hair."

All the adults burst out laughing, and the boy reddened.

"See? You should get it cut," Jean teased. Henry shook his head.

"So, you retraced their steps and found us here," Lilly concluded.

"Yes. It took a while."

"I should say. Why would you put so much effort into one man?"

"Lilly," Santino said, leaning forward. "You have no idea who this man is, really. Maybe you don't want to know."

"Maybe not," Lilly said.

"He's a famous man. Well, infamous is the word, I guess."

Jean sat looking at Lilly on the far side of the table. His eyes were set, with no apology. He simply wanted her to know, to understand.

"Ma'am," Santino continued. "All that aside, this man gave up his whole life for you, for your kids."

Lilly smiled. He was right. They were right. No matter what darkened their past, what was here and now was most important, a blessing, a connection, the love of a man. Santino reached into his pocket and produced his wallet. His fingers struggled through the cards and found the photo, which he handed to Lilly.

"I love this photo," she said. "We took it down on the beach. You're right, there's a boat in the background."

She handed the photo across to Jean, who took it and looked long at it.

"I never thought I would see this again. Thank you, my friend," he said to Santino.

A comfortable silence followed. All the meeting's members fell to contemplation of the weighty conversation. Henry, with a boy's curiosity, was the next to speak.

"So, what about killing Jean LaChance?"

"Yes, that's the important part. My friend, Guy and I have come up with the perfect solution to our little conundrum," Jean said.

"You see," he was talking to Lilly again. "Santino came here to arrest me. When we took off in the Jeep, I thought killing him was the only way out. We drove to the end of the side road. That was my plan. I couldn't see any other way. Santino was working with the FBI."

"The fucking FBI?" Lilly cried.

"Yes, the fucking FBI," Jean said. Henry laughed. "I believe that's their technical name. So, Santino had to save his skin. There was no other way. He loves his life too much to die."

LaChance threw back the rest of his wine and held his glass up for more. Lilly poured the remainder of the bottle.

"I guess we'll need another one."

She got up from the chair, and Jean could see she was shaking.

"Lilly, Lilly it's okay," he said.

"I know, I know. It's just a lot to digest, this whole thing. And I'm thinking everyday about changing diapers and fixing lunch."

"That's good. Somebody has to think about lunch," Jean said. Santino laughed.

Lilly brought a new bottle back to the table. Jean beckoned her to his side. He slid his chair back from the table, and pulled her down onto his lap, kissing her deeply. She smiled at him and poured the wine, poured some for Santino and hesitated a bit before pouring Henry another half inch.

"Thanks, Mom."

"This is a special treat, honey. You hear me?"

"Yeah."

"We talked about it. There was no other way. Somebody had to die, so we decided it might as well be Jean LaChance," Jean said.

"How is that going to happen?" Lilly asked Santino.

"Well, I can get some hair from his head, take his prints, run a DNA test with it when I get back, something like that. His passport, any identification that says Jean LaChance. We'll come up with a story that will be credible. They'll believe me. I have a good record."

"Glad you brought that up, Guy," Lilly said. What about your oath?"

Santino smiled wryly and took a swig from the glass.

"I'm a private dick now, Lilly. I retired from the police force. Technically, I'm no longer under any oath."

"I see. And your ethics? Not that I want him arrested. Just want you to explain yourself."

"Well, as Jean said, my other option was to die on a small island in the Caribbean and feed fish for the next month. The other thing is that I've done this a long time, Lilly. There's so much badness, both inside and outside the law. This man," he put a finger on LaChance's chest. "This is not a bad man."

"No, he isn't," Lilly said, kissing his forehead.

"If I call the FBI, they will come here and get him, dead or alive. It would serve no Earthly purpose to put him behind bars, and besides," he paused to make a point, "that would destroy your lives."

Santino sat back in his chair.

"I was a police officer. I didn't take the oath to destroy people's lives. Jean is living here now, part of the community. Prescott's money served to rebuild this community. That fat bastard just kept it hidden under his bed. Taking it from him and using it like this is justice."

They clinked glasses again and Lilly filled them with the end of the bottle.

"There's just one matter that was never resolved," Santino said gravely.

"What's that?" Jean asked.

Santino gestured with his finger toward LaChance.

"Who killed Dewey Jensen?"

The question struck the festive table like a lightning bolt. Dewey. They had forgotten about Dewey.

"I did," Jean and Henry answered at the same time.

The surprise of the man-boy chorus, perfectly timed, sent a silence into the thick air that was immediately followed by nervous laughter from the adults.

"I did," Henry said again. He dropped his head until his dreadlocks touched the table. "I hated him. I shot him with my .22. He was never gonna hurt my mother again."

Santino, Jean and Lilly all sat looking at the child who had killed Dewey Jensen. Henry looked up through dreadlocks that had fallen across his face smeared with tears. Lilly reached over and stroked his head. They all sat in silence for a time.

"Don't worry about it, kid," Santino finally said. "I don't think that guy deserved to live, from what I've heard." He laid a hand on Henry's shoulder. "And it was self-defense in your own house."

"He did do one good thing," LaChance said.

"What's that?" Lilly asked.

"If you think about it, we would never have met if not for Dewey Jensen."

They all considered this last statement. Slowly, Jean raised his glass and offered it in the air.

"To Dewey Jensen," he toasted.

"Dewey Jensen," the others echoed, and the glasses struck mid-table.

Chapter 39

Amos crept down the stairs clutching baby Evie to his hip. The sight of the stranger snoring on the sitting room sofa froze his foot mid-step. A feeling of danger seeped through his skin and sat weighty on his chest. Distant memories flashed through his brain; he knew the man from somewhere.

He twisted toward the railing and ascended the stairs again, padded in bare feet to his parents' bedroom door and pressed his ear against it. Steady snoring. Knocking softly, he pushed the door open a crack. A tousled curly head lifted from the right pillow. Lilly had always been a light sleeper.

"Hey buddy," she whispered. "Come here."

Amos smiled. The joy of being summoned to his mother's bed never diminished. Evie squealed slightly as he placed her up on the high mattress next to her mother. Lilly kissed the baby and patted the bed next to her, shifting her weight to accommodate Amos.

Amos jumped up beside the baby and kissed his mother. The good son. He never complained, never talked back, never caused a problem of any kind. At times, Amos was virtually invisible. His quiet, unassuming nature occupied a deep, enigmatic place within the structure of the family. He didn't seem to need attention at all, but yet performed the gargantuan task of raising Evie with little instruction. Lilly knew she had to appreciate him more.

"Mom, there's a guy sleeping downstairs," Amos said. "I think I know him."

"You do, honey."

"Who is he?"

"Remember Detective Santino? From Tucson?"

"The guy who took you to the airport?" The fright showed in his eyes. He would never forget the guy who took his mother away.

"Yeah. That's him."

The boy's eyes jumped open wide.

"When did he get here?"

"Yesterday. Don't worry, honey. Everything's okay. Your father's got it all figured out."

"Wow," Amos said. "Dad's not leaving again, is he?"

"No! No, honey, everything is alright."

She lifted her hand and stroked his hair.

"You can go downstairs if you want to. Is Sherri awake?"

"Not yet."

"You want to go get the eggs?"

"Sure."

"Thank you, my sweet boy."

"You're welcome. 'Morning, Dad."

The snoring had abruptly stopped as Jean opened his eyes. He raised himself on one elbow.

"'Morning, buddy. I'll take Evie."

"Thanks, Dad. I'll get the eggs. Should I wake Sherri?"

"No, no that's okay. Let her sleep."

Jean hoisted the baby over Lilly and set her on his chest. The child let out a shriek at the sight of her father that rocked the intensity of the hangover in his skull. He smiled through the pain at the vision of his love child.

He threw his right arm over Lilly's head and pulled her in for a kiss to her temple.

"Merci," she said.

"De rien."

Lilly stretched back, wishing the coffee would make itself, then come to the bedroom with a bottle of aspirin. The hot pokers behind her eyes punished her for the anxious consumption of wine.

"Got a little drunk last night, mmmm?" he teased.

"How do you feel?"

"Not bad, considering. Margaret finally pushed us out the door. We were pretty loaded."

"Yes, you were," Lilly jabbed. "By the way, where's the Jeep?"

"Parked at the Hot Spot. I have to get a ride up there today."

"And then?"

"And then, my love, we're going to drive to the far side of the island and bury Jean LaChance."

"Oh, my God, that's right. That's the last thing we talked about last night. You were serious?"

"Damn right. It was Santino's idea."

"Really?"

"Yeah."

She snuggled against his shoulder and played a finger game with Evie.

"Jean?"

"Mmmmm?"

"Would you have killed him?"

The Frenchman kissed the top of her head. Thank Christ it hadn't gone that way.

"Yes, if I had to. There was no other solution. But he didn't call the cops or tell the FBI. He was armed, but didn't pull a gun. It was strange."

"What was strange?"

"I think he just wanted to meet and talk. I really do. He wanted to solve the crime. All men have egos. It's tough to fail."

"He seems like a good man."

"He is."

"That whole thing yesterday made me so nervous."

He tightened his grip on her shoulder.

"I'm sorry, Lilly. It made me nervous, too. I'm not a killer."

"I always knew that about you."

"Yeah? That's good. Even from the beginning?"

"Even from the beginning. Doesn't mean you don't look dangerous with that cannon in your hand."

LaChance laughed.

"It's not such a big gun."

"Looked big to me."

"I have it here, you know."

"What?" Lilly sat up and looked at him.

"Yeah, my friend sent it to me a couple of months ago. It's always good to have a gun, Lilly."

"I guess so."

"I took it with me yesterday. I just wanted Santino to know I would do it if he pushed. I'm glad he didn't push."

"Wow."

"Speaking of Santino, let's get up and see how our guest feels today."

"Ohhhh," Lilly groaned.

Jean reached over and squeezed her breast playfully.

"We have lots of time for that, girl. We have plenty to do today."

"Well, what a change you've made."

"Not really. I would love to stay here with you all day and make love. But we have our first guest in the house."

"That's right," Lilly said.

She watched him stretch out of bed, his muscular arms raised above his head, his nakedness like a marble statue. She realized how lucky she was and that the painful, lonely years of her life before meeting this man had all been a worthy trade for the contentment she now felt.

Jean pulled on a pair of pants and turned to take the baby from Lilly's side.

"I love you," he said.

"I love you too, Pierre," she joked.

"That's not necessary."

"Why? Aren't we going to bury LaChance today?"

He smiled.

"Not necessary," he repeated, and whisked Evie to his shoulders and out the door.

Santino was snoring like a water buffalo on the sofa. Jean changed Evie, cooing about her wet diaper and how beautiful she was in the morning. Evie touched his face with her chubby fingers. The back screen door squeaked as Amos brought the eggs into the kitchen. He set the basket on the counter and came to claim his charge from his father.

Standing side by side at the changing table, father and son descended into adolescent babble with little Evie, lying on her back, smiling at the private show put on by her two favorite people in the entire world. Jean reached over to the top of Amos' head and kissed it. Amos looked up with a shy boy smile.

"You do such a good job with her, buddy."

"Thanks, Dad. She's my sister."

Evie squealed at the momentary lapse of attention. They both looked down.

"Is everything okay?" Amos asked.

Jean embraced the boy with one arm and hugged him tight.

"Everything's just fine," the man said. "Do you think we should have another baby?"

The boy's face reddened.

"I don't know. I like having Evie here. She's starting to walk really good now and talks all the time."

"What you're doing with her is very important," Jean said.

"Yeah? I just play with her."

"It's very important. You're such a good boy."

"Mom always says that."

"She means it."

The snoring in the next room was suddenly interrupted by snorts and a cough.

"Sounds like our guest is awake," Jean said.

He passed through to the kitchen, glancing in the sitting room to see Santino propped up on the sofa, holding his head with both hands.

"'Morning, Guy," Jean said.

"Arrrgggghhh," Santino groaned. "Gettin' too old for this shit."

Jean started the coffee and poured Santino a glass of water. When he came into the room, the man was sitting smiling at Amos and the baby on the other sofa. LaChance handed him the water.

"Thanks, man."

He drank it to the bottom and expelled a breath heavily.

"Ahhhhhhhh. That's better."

"You remember Amos."

"Yes, I do, but I don't think I ever heard him say anything."

Amos smiled shyly.

"And this is Evie," Jean introduced them.

"Lilly's mother's name?"

"Yeah."

"Ever meet her?" Santino asked.

"No."

"You're a lucky man."

The men laughed.

"I was shocked when I met Lilly. She's so beautiful to have such a troll for a mother."

"They don't talk at all."

"I heard."

"That was quite a little party last night."

"Jesus."

"We didn't eat anything, either," Jean said.

"I know. What idiots, huh? Amos, don't ever do that."

"He will. Just give him time."

Lilly descended the open staircase. She was Esther Williams, Vivian Leigh, Bette Davis. Santino watched her come down the steps. She came to the sofa and kissed the tops of Jean's and Amos' heads and took the baby.

"I'll get breakfast," she said, and disappeared into the kitchen. Amos got up and followed his mother. He had no words for the stranger in the house.

"You lucky bastard," Santino said.

"I am. Do you have kids?"

"Two. They live with their mother and step-father."

"That's too bad."

"Yeah. I see them almost every weekend. I think it would've gone differently if I had gotten married later, like you."

Jean nodded.

"Yes, it certainly changed my life."

"You miss it?"

"Are you nuts? Well, there are some things. I love the adrenalin. I miss the planning, the strategy. But most of it, no. It was a lonely life. I didn't know that until I met Lilly."

As on cue, she appeared at the door of the kitchen.

"Guy, how do you take your coffee?"

"Black, from a beautiful woman."

Lilly smiled. "I can do both of those things."

A sudden thumping came from the back door, and Henry appeared on the back steps lugging a huge bag of citrus fruit. He had been up for hours. He dumped it on the floor and came into the room to join the men.

"'Morning, Dad. 'Morning, Mr. Santino."

"'Morning," both men replied.

"Ramón has lots of fruit. His trees survived really well. We're going to dig up some of the saplings from near his property and plant them here."

"Good idea," Jean said.

"I told him we wouldn't be working on the house today, so he spread the word."

"Oh, thanks."

"I figured with Mr. Santino here, we would be busy."

"Yes, we have a funeral to plan," Santino joked.

"You know, you're welcome to stay for a while," Jean said to Santino.

"I do love this place."

Death of the Frenchman

"Nothing to hurry back to, is there?"
"Not really. My kids. I guess that's it."
"If you can operate a hammer, we could use the hands."
"I'll think about that."

Lilly came in with three cups of steaming coffee, which she set down on a table. Jean pulled her down onto his lap. Amos dragged the baby in by her hand and sat on the floor. The day of Jean LaChance's funeral had begun.

Death of the Frenchman

Chapter 40

The Jeep hurtled down the narrow road to the far side of the island, packed full with Jean and Lilly's family and Santino; children occupying all the adult laps except for Jean, who was driving. It was May, and the trade winds were surrendering their strength to tropic summer. The day was growing hot; a perfect day for a swim. A huge basket of sandwiches, fruit and drinks rode in the back near the spare. Scraps was squeezed in next to it on the folded blankets, his ears flapping like a cartoon character.

Laughter filled the open vehicle. Peace settled over the little crowd on their way to bury the man who had brought them all together.

The afternoon melted away into kids' games filled with splashing sea water and sand castles, and finally, at four o'clock, they packed up the basket and walked above the high water line.

Henry had prepared a make-shift driftwood head stone that read Jean LaChance, born Paris, France, February 27, 1943, died May 15, 1994. Together, they mounded the sandy soil onto the body-sized grave site, which they lined with small stones, and dug a hole for the headstone. Everyone stood around the grave site, feeling the eerie sensation of the funeral ritual, though no one had actually died.

"That's macabre," Jean finally said, to break the silence.

"Seeing your name on a headstone?" Lilly asked.

"Yeah, it's a little creepy."

"Well, here's to Jean LaChance," Santino said. "May he rest in peace."

"He is at peace," Jean said, his arm wrapped around Lilly.

The funeral had reached its conclusion, and Lilly and the kids headed back toward the Jeep. Jean stood looking at the grave. Santino stayed with him. Jean produced a pack of cigarettes and shook two out. The men lit up and stood smoking in silence.

"Any regrets?" Santino finally asked.

Jean pursed his lips and thought a while.

"Really none that I can think of. Maybe the death of my mother. It would be good to have her around. But then, my life would have been totally different. Who knows? I might be a doctor or a lawyer right now."

Santino laughed.

"I think you're doing just fine, my friend."

My friend. Jean smiled at the irony. He reached over the grave and extended his hand to the man who had pursued him relentlessly for over two years. The men shook hands. They ground out their cigarettes and started back for the Jeep.

"I could use you here," LaChance said.

"I'll think about it. I have to go home for a while. There's always my kids."

"Kids are important," LaChance mused.

"Very important."

"Very, very important."

Beyond the reach of the endless sea, the horizon beckoned the sun on its way down to the end of the Earth. With the sunset in its rearview mirrors, the Jeep made its way back to the house.

Chapter 41

LaChance drove Santino to the airstrip on a balmy morning two weeks after the funeral on the beach. The trip was full of a sadness they couldn't express. Two men, who once had been mortal enemies were now friends. They smoked and drove. Conversation was limited to every meaningless passing scene unrelated to their errand. The wind blew in from every direction behind the windscreen of the Jeep, whipping their faces and bodies with the tropical sun-kissed air that was everyday life on the island. They were free. The word meant different things to Jean and Santino, but both knew on their own level the essence of freedom.

As much as the men could experience sadness, both of the men felt deeply sad to be mile by mile separating themselves from the freedom they felt in the Jeep, from each other. That morning, they ate breakfast. They gathered eggs and took a walk around the property. Lilly cried. The kids hugged Santino.

The kids' emotion was unimaginable to the adults. They had been terrified of Santino. He was the One Who Had Been After Them all. He had hunted them. He had put his hands on Lilly. He had used the intimidation of government muscle. In two weeks, he had become a trusted friend and a guest in their house. Black to white. Cold to hot. If there was confusion, it didn't show.

Jean and Santino shared a special bond. Every night passed with laughter. Every day was hard physical work on the guest house; plans made, construction progressed, promises solidified. The men forged a relationship born of conflict into one forged on trust.

No one wanted to see Santino go.

Life goes on, they said. No one gets everything they want. Every night when they drank and ate together, they teased, laughed and simply lived life. Every morning they woke, greeted the morning, and helped each other. This was the way life was supposed to be.

A few passengers waited the airport. Santino joined the line and checked in. Jean sat outside in the Jeep. He wished things could be different, but had spent a lifetime of these moments. He was used to it.

Santino exited the building and joined LaChance. The plane would leave in thirty minutes. They chose a last drink at the Hot Spot.

Margaret was predictably behind the bar. She knew the men were coming. The drunken night when Santino arrived at the island had made her privy to their story. She knew something about the circumstances behind the visit of Mr. Pierre's "friend," and the course it could have taken, but didn't; lives that could have been ruined, but weren't. She was always there, and ready to help when she could. She knew the difference between reality and fantasy.

The men drank shots, ordered another, stood and smoked and drank and used the precious moments remaining until the flight boarded. Jean and Santino shook hands, then embraced, kisses to cheeks and slaps to backs, and then the American was gone, and the Frenchman remained alone inside the bar, sitting at the table, smoking.

Margaret gave him quite a while to himself. Mr. Pierre was that kind of man. She knew that kind of man. Stoic, passionate, dedicated, loving, full of life. She waited and watched until she was sure.

"Mr. Pierre?"

"Yes?"

"I would like to buy you a drink."

"Thank you, Margaret."

She produced two shot glasses and filled them with tequila.

She lifted one and gestured to the Frenchman to take the other. Jean picked up the shot and waited, glass in mid-air.

"To life, no matter how confusing it may seem. Life happens to us all, in time. May we all learn from every minute."

"Salud," the Frenchmen said. They toasted over the bar, and the sound of the ascending prop plane drowned out the clink of the glasses.

About the Author

Barbara lives in Gloucester, MA with her jazz drummer and sailor husband, Al Boudreau. Together, they play and record with their jazz band. They live on their sailboat *Catitude* in the summer on a mooring in Gloucester Harbor and dream of sailing away upon retirement, which can't come soon enough. By day, she works as an Interpretive Coordinator for Mass State Parks and is a Certified Interpretive Guide Instructor. Her love of nature and all things wild led to an educational background in Fish and Wildlife and Natural Resources. She has published articles about conservation, interpretation and sailing and her first novel *The Frenchman* in 2013. She writes daily with the company of her very old but loyal dog, Lila.